THE CARBON CONSPIRACY

A Novel By
Stuart Murphy

ISBN: 1483916871
ISBN 13: 9781483916873
Library of Congress Control Number: 2013905442
CreateSpace Independent Publishing Platform
North Charleston, South Carolina

George Murphy, who inspired my lifelong love of reading

ACKNOWLEDGEMENT

I'm thankful for the enduring love and support of my wife, Sharon, and our children. In particular I wish to acknowledge, with gratitude, the critical review of various drafts offered by Christina Riehman-Murphy and Lauren Murphy whose insight and suggestions were immensely valuable.

ONE

"I'd like to speak with Mark Burnham as soon as possible about a matter of considerable importance." The woman's voice is charged with emotion. If she gets past Shauna, I know I'm in for an earful.

Passion either bores me or scares me. When I meet with a male lobbyist, it's like confronting my alter ego. Within five minutes, I'm ready either to kick the bum out or spend the evening with him downing beers engaged in the endless trash-talking guys love. But the women? They have just the right look—facial expressions and voices dripping with sincerity so profound that you're ready to open your heart and, of more importance to them, your bank account to win their approval.

When she walks in it's a whole different ball game. Every encounter is with someone from your past—that unattainable girlfriend from high school; the button-pusher who conjures up visions of you wringing her neck; your mother consoling, correcting, or scolding; or that nirvana most men secretly want: the women they can share their most intimate thoughts without romance or sex mucking up the relationship.

Which one is she? Who knows? As always, the internal battle rears its head. On the one hand, I know that nine visitors out of ten will want something I can't deliver. Yet I must say the right words to convince them that they have gained some level of influence over the congressman, my boss. That one in ten keeps my hope alive. Years of experience have not dulled the gender effect, but have taught me to listen beyond the words, sifting what's real from the mountains of fluff moving from their mouths to my ears. That diamond in the rough is the person who offers some valuable tidbit of information in support of the ever-present goal of every staffer: reelection of his member of congress.

In general, the public has no idea I exist. As staff director to the most powerful member of Congress on environmental issues, Congressman Tom Trendle representing California's 56 district, I wield enormous power while remaining anonymous to outsiders and admired (or feared) by insiders. For as long I can remember, my father, Art Burnham, challenged me never to accept anything or anyone at face value. "Probe, prod, and pound if necessary to get to the heart of the matter," he drummed into me. "Trust is a treasure given sparingly to only a few." That advice has served me well in Congress. The result is a cultivation of many acquaintances with trust reserved for a select few.

To the average voter, all power rests with his very visible congressional representative, who spends every spare moment kissing babies, seeking supporters and replenishing his reelection account with dollars, dollars, and more dollars. I relish the lack of public notoriety. My one-bedroom apartment is three blocks from the Capitol on the third floor of an old but well-kept brownstone. Even Trendle probably doesn't know or care where I live, and that's fine with me. We staffers quietly make our way to and from the Hill daily, exchanging pleasantries and boatloads of gossip among us.

Congressional offices are worse than a bus station. They're an endless parade of visitors stopping by, hoping to get something from their representative. As Congressman Trendle's chief of staff, it's my job to ensure that office protocol is followed. Because of our visibility as environmental watchdogs, the office resembles an emergency room after a train wreck. Visitors are triaged based on the urgency of the issue; their prominence; and most important, on their potential impact on Trendle's polling numbers.

I'm in my usual pose: shirtsleeves rolled up, tie askew, leftover lunch container on the desk as I digest a request from an influential lobbyist who nurtures numerous channels for legally pouring money into Trendle's reelection coffers. It doesn't matter that we violently disagree with the request. Money talks and Trendle has charged me with finding a way to appease this guy without completely abandoning our principles.

The voice of the unseen visitor reaches my ears from the reception area. Her intensity is such that it distracts me from the matter at hand.

"May I ask what the issue is?"

"It's in regards to the environment."

Ha. Probably another advocate wanting to remind us that the world is about to choke on an overload of carbon. As if I didn't know. While much of a staffer's work is behind the scenes, my passion for the environment is well known among insiders. My apartment has a magnificent view of the Capitol dome and yet all too often, I'm distracted by the pollution that hangs in the air tarnishing the view. That makes me angry, as do self-serving fakes pretending to be in love with clean air. Visitors have to convince me of their environmental credentials before I let them anywhere near Trendle.

"Unfortunately, he's unavailable," Shauna says, "but if you leave some information I'm sure he'll review it."

I really do want to maintain an open-door policy, but the reality of political life is this: There are too many favor-seekers asking for too much from politicians, and a system that has too few perks to meet the insatiable demand.

There is a quiet force to her voice that smacks of anxiety, even fear. Perhaps she has something worthwhile to share. However, I'm up to my neck with work, and with back-to-back meetings, I simply don't have the time.

The day started out on a low and has been heading downhill ever since. At 5:45 a.m., a call jerked me out of bed and a deceptively pleasant female voice informed me that my credit score is a mess and the bank is threatening to call in my auto loan. Annoyed that any bill collector would call me, much less at an illegal hour of the day, ensured I was pissed even before arriving at work. Between morning meetings, I managed to squeeze in the five calls it took to discover that the credit rating agency in question had bad information, apparently due to identity theft. Once straightened out, I'd normally have put the incident behind me, but the caller knew too much about my personal life and now that's nagging at the edge of my conscious. Where did she find out about the arrest for underage drinking at a high school homecoming celebration? The misdemeanor was eventually expunged and all but forgotten, or so I thought. If anything, that experience taught me a valuable lesson in managing alcohol. The information should not be on anybody's radar much less that of a collection firm. My anger becomes tinged with paranoia when an Internet search reveals that the bill collector doesn't exist.

As I'm about to head home, after another 14 hour day, our long suffering office manager, Shauna, pops her head in. "I need to speak with you!" I almost brush her off but change my mind after one look at the concern on her face. "Shauna what's on your mind?"

"This morning a woman came by insisting that she needed to meet with you about an environmental issue. Thinking back I recall overhearing the conversation. "Yeah, I remember she sounded anxious."

"She was, her name is Connie Imlen and after she left I looked her up on Google. You won't believe what I found!"

Shauna instincts are good and if she thought it worthwhile to check her out I better listen so I nodded for her to continue.

"Connie Imlen is, or rather was, the foremost expert on nuclear power plant accidents and apparently not afraid to speak out when she felt the public needed to know about a potential danger. Over the years she has rubbed both industry and members of Congress the wrong way."

"What do you mean", I interrupted.

"She was willing go over her boss's head more than once and inform the press about serious safety matters that those who should have cared would rather have swept under the carpet." "How serious" I ask?

"Enough that there was the potential for mass casualties" she replied.

I'm beginning to regret not meeting with her. I look up at Shauna and can see from her expression that there is more. "What else".

"Based on old news articles I could find important papers were stolen from her hotel room right before a meeting she had scheduled with the press regarding a major nuclear incident back in the 60s. She also received an anonymous death threat."

"What did the police say?"

"It looks like they brushed the threat off as a crank letter. The cops hit a dead end on the hotel theft and dropped the whole thing."

"Shauna, get in touch with Ms. Imlen and schedule an appointment as soon as possible."

TWO

As my attention drifts away from the speaker across from me I glance at a flier some wit, a staffer for one of the members from Texas, printed up and circulated to all the congressional offices. To relieve pressure we staffers launch endless gags targeting each other. This week I'm on the receiving end.

"Meet Mark Burnham; single white mail, age 32, average height, slim, athletic, with chiseled features seeking fun loving girl who enjoys, long hours, constant pressure, low pay, and endless political intrigue. She must have low expectations, be comfortable with constant interruptions as I text and talk at all hours on my cell and when we are on a date likely to fall asleep in the middle of a conversation."

I'm laughing to myself because it's true. This job is all consuming and leaves little time for romance.

Jolted back to reality by the visitor across from me who's really getting wound up I drop the flier in the trash.

"Mark, the situation is clear, carbon levels have been steadily increasing over the past century. At the same time, the mean temperature has dramatically risen around the globe. Industrialization is the cause and the United States the principal villain," says Bennett Longworth, a professor at the University of Michigan. To me he's just another smarmy professor living off grants to fund endless research and a responsibility-free lifestyle. If it were up to me, I wouldn't spend any time with him, but Trendle insisted.

The professor is undoubtedly hurting us on the Internet with negative information he sends out on social networking sites. Trendle doesn't know a tweet from a twit, but he knows guys like Longworth are reaching young voters in ways he never dreamed possible. Every week I hear from someone else throwing a quote from Longworth in my face. We're facing off in the cramped conference room, surrounded by stacks of briefs, congressional testimony, and correspondence from supporters and detractors alike. Sitting around the table with Professor Longworth are three of his graduate students, dressed in de facto university uniforms: jeans, T-shirts and Converse sneakers. At first, I wasn't clear why the professor brought them. While he's speaking, their demeanors and attitudes project distrust, disbelief, and arrogance at my every response, especially when I challenge the professor's facts.

Then it dawns on me that they serve as a kind of visual performance designed to add drama to his oratory. After ten minutes of their snickers and mumbled remarks about lying politicians, I've finally had it. He and his entourage are the ninth visitor I've met with so far today and my patience is gone.

"Professor, you asked for this meeting. If your students are incapable of mature behavior, perhaps we should end it now."

One of them, a young woman filled with zeal, fires back in a voice laced with sarcasm. "You'd better get on the web. Everyone knows about the carbon snow job you and Trendle are foisting on the American public!"

I have a dozen retorts ready, including a cutting comment regarding her lack of hygiene, but thankfully, before I can tell her where to shove the attitude, Longworth intervenes. "Betsy, let me handle this."

With that, she shuts her mouth and the three of them sit back, sulking in silence.

"While perhaps overzealous, Betsy is correct," Longworth says, pointing his finger directly at me. "You and Trendle are nothing more than conspirators who prop up the oil industry while pretending to support renewable energy."

I'm about ready to slap him. PhD or not, I'm confident that the years of reviewing information from thousands of experts and listening to endless arguments from both sides of the aisle ensures I'm better prepared to judge what's relevant than this guy is.

"I track the blogs," Longworth continues. "Your political backers are a bunch of wealthy do-gooders who never give a thought to the fact that each of their 25,000-square-foot homes produces more greenhouse gases than the headquarters of the American Coal Association."

He exaggerates, but not by much. It's a sore point with me that our wealthiest supporters are among the worst abusers of carbon. They talk a good line and some even pay a carbon offset, but the fact remains that if push comes to shove, they'll opt for the convenience of fossil-fueled luxury cars, boats, and private jets every time. Of course, since wealth trumps everything, our rich donors honestly don't see a contradiction. Wealth has its privileges.

"They talk like environmentalists but sit on boards of companies that pour tons of carbon into the atmosphere."

As passionate as I am about the environment, it's frustrating to watch extremists on both sides of the issue spend endless energy pointing fingers and accusing the other side of corruption and payoffs. Longworth irritates me for another reason, too: He reminds me too much of myself in both appearance and demeanor. He's pretentious, possessing all the right attributes of a university don: tall, thin (borderline gaunt), with wavy hair carefully arranged to look like it's never combed, and he's wearing jeans, penny loafers, a plaid shirt, a striped tie, and a corduroy jacket.

Though I've never been a professor, I can be pretty arrogant in any debate related to global warming and the evils of Big Oil. On the other hand, the clothing thing is purely accidental. I generally don't realize what I'm wearing until I get home in the evening. While I may have a vague consciousness that an ensemble doesn't match, in truth I don't care. As it turns out, neither do the women I've dated over the years. They like the borderline over-confident attitude and figure they can fix the fashion disaster once they get me to the altar. Disillusionment inevitably sets in when they discover that environment and politics will always be my first loves.

Most staffers eventually surrender to the lure of money and regular hours. The work is exhilarating, but years of long days and the continuous emotional roller coaster of being on both ends of unrelenting political finger-pointing, the survival panic at every election cycle, and the pitifully low pay drives many staffers to call it quits and become what they long despised: a corporate slug, or worse, a lobbyist. Thankfully, I haven't reached that point. When I do, my hope is to run for office or accept an influential appointment at the Environmental Protection Agency.

I'm rising from my chair ready to get in his face when the professor abruptly gets up and with a disapproving look, throws a printout from an article in yesterday's Washington Post on the table as he and his students slither out.

Looking at the headline, I seethe with anger. Their type is tone-deaf to the realities of politics and gullible in believing the most outrageous lies.

Environmental Whistleblower Murdered for Speaking the Truth ?

Suddenly a nagging fear rears up. I quickly bring up the article online and am devastated to learn the whistleblower is non-other than Connie Imlen. I'm full of self-recrimination.

"Why didn't I meet with her the other day?"

The article suggests that the circumstances of her death are such that murder is being considered by the police.

THREE

Congressional hearings, born out of crisis, are an art form all to themselves. They demand careful planning, a clear understanding of the goal, and a healthy dose of luck. They are the battleground of choice for Congressman Tom Trendle, foremost champion of renewable energy, enemy of the oil industry, and my boss.

At first blush, he possesses none of the qualities normally associated with a successful politician. He's in his early seventies, homely, with oversized ears, an abnormally turned up nose, and odd strands of hair pasted every which way on top of what is otherwise a barren landscape. With a signature nasal twang that endears him to friends and strikes fear into the heart of his enemies, he has turned a non-telegenic liability into an asset. When Trendle aims his righteous rage and dripping sarcasm at an enemy, he takes on the aura of an avenging angel ready to lay waste to anything and anyone who gets in his way.

As chairman of the House Energy and Commerce Committee, Trendle's well positioned to strike at his opponents. There's no one in Congress greener than Trendle. He's a constant thorn in the side of the business community. His district is so engaged in the environment that he can be as far left of center as he wants. It only energizes his base.

An oil company, public enemy number one, just handed us the golden egg with its latest oil spill. A hearing's inevitable.

"Mark, I need you to get on top of this. Drop everything else you're working on." What Trendle really wants from me is every piece of dirt I can uncover that can be used as ammunition during the hearing.

A recurring theme of ours is focusing on second-tier oil companies. With the professor's stinging assault on my integrity still scratching at my conscience, I decide to challenge Trendle.

"Why do we target the smaller producers and let the multinationals slide?" He pauses, runs his hand over his forehead, and stares at me long enough that I become uncomfortable.

"Mark, you should know better," he finally says. "We can score quick hits against outfits like Pierson, who, I might add, is not all that small. The big boys' political clout is such that even as chairman, I'd be waging an uphill battle with senior congressmen from the oil states throwing up procedural hurdles at every turn."

His explanation makes perfect sense and yet, as I make my way home for the night, I suspect it also has something to do with his wealthy supporters whose palatial West Coast estates offer them majestic views of the Pacific. They may ooze green in public, but much of their wealth still flows from mainline industries that rely on traditional energy sources.

Junk mail is nothing new. I'm inundated daily, as marketers must be under the illusion that Hill staffers have the time, interest, or money to buy their products. As I pop open a beer and engage in the evening ritual of flipping through the envelopes before tossing them, my fingers stop at an advertisement for free credit-score services. It cites the mythical example of a family losing everything because of bad credit. Can it be a coincidence that this hypothetical family is from the same small, Midwestern town where my parents almost lost their home due to a real-estate investment scam? This, on top of the early morning call the other day from the phony bill collector, confirms I'm on somebody's radar, but why?

"Good morning, friends!" says Trendle, cheerfully greeting us at the ungodly hour of 6 a.m. as we stumble into his conference room to prep for the hearing.

The target of our investigation is Pierson Petroleum. It was Pierson's leased ship that leaked the oil. Chairman and longtime CEO Win Blankenphal, an intense, ruddy individual in his early sixties who wildcatted in his younger days, brought a success-driven ego to Pierson. He took the risk of hunting for oil and gas in the lower forty-eight states right before energy prices shot through the roof. He cashed out when oil prices were at their peak by selling profitable but hard-to-work fields to the majors. When prices dropped, as he knew they would, the big boys were stuck with unprofitable fields while Pierson continued to squeeze a nice return from the far more efficient ones he retained. As business-savvy as he is, Blankenphal is known to be a hothead. If we push the right buttons, he'll do the rest.

The hearing, scheduled for April 21, is guaranteed to command national attention and offers opportunities beyond the issue itself. The benefits are incalculable. It will energize Trendle's base and boost the flow of money into his reelection coffers. With oil as the target, we hit pay dirt.

"The WW9 will love this," laughs Trendle. "Mark, when this is over I'll need you to fly out to the West Coast and share with them every juicy detail that emerges."

The Wise and Wealthy Nine are Trendle's wealthiest and most faithful political supporters. And naturally, they in turn will leak the good news in whispered conversations to their closest friends—left-leaning artists, musicians, exclusive clothing designers, several owners of upscale boutiques, and a few large vineyard masters who produce a limited number of outstanding bottles. Since the WW9 are feeding the money into Trendle's reelection treasure chest, no effort is spared to meet their need for attention.

Trendle can't help himself. Like a little kid, he keeps clapping his hands and saying to whoever will listen, "Don't you just love it?"

And I do. While professing outrage, deep down I relish an oil spill, and the closer to beachfront property, the better. It assures maximum press coverage, public outrage from the environmentalists, and reinforces Trendle's supremacy as the House champion of renewable energy. All this is music to my ears. I love the edgy energy of politics, and prepping for an assault on oil is like pumping adrenaline mixed with steroids straight into my jugular. I'm primed and ready to rumble.

As soon as the hearing is announced, friends of Big Oil are all over Trendle. Hempforth of Texas, a fellow Democrat, barges into his office. For the next thirty minutes, the sounds of angry voices and desk-pounding are heard. Suddenly, the door flies open and a red-faced and clearly frustrated Hempforth stomps out. They have been engaged in secret negotiations for months, with me as a go-between. Trendle wants the Texas delegation's support for increased mileage requirements for the auto industry, and Hempforth is looking for Trendle's quiet support for expanded drilling on federal land in Texas. The hearing threatens to derail the talks.

"Aren't you concerned about opposition from pro-oil Democrats?" I ask.

With a smirk that broadens into a smile, Trendle replies, "My boy, if they're that worried, it means we hit pay dirt. The hearing will make us look like prophets of a bright future and the oil industry, a bunch of greedy, out-of-touch rednecks." After a pause he looks me in the eye, and lowering his voice, says, "Don't tell anyone this, but the part I enjoy most is the squirming and double-talk about responsibility to shareholders the oil executives engage in to avoid what they really want to say: 'Shit happens whenever eight-seven million barrels of oil are moved and consumed everyday around the world.'"

The hearing's focus is on the recent spill of two thousand gallons of heavy crude off Bayonne, New Jersey. Because horseshoe crabs were photographed covered with oil, it was picked up by *The New York Times* and featured on CNN's, *The Situation Room*. The art of the hearing requires several ingredients, all of which are present. The oily oil executives are the opening act, followed by a couple of marine biologists who will passionately testify on the scientific and emotional impact on the crabs. Throw in the chairwomen of New Jerseyians for Clean Beaches and the bureaucrat from the EPA, and the circus is in full swing. The fact that Earth Day is the day after the hearing begins is icing on the cake.

As Trendle's about to leave for a fund-raising dinner, he pops his head into my office. "Hey Mark, I just thought of something."

I know him well enough to know he never just thinks of something.

"That reporter friend of yours…what's his name?"

"You mean Josh Adams?

"Yeah, that's the one." Trendle knows his name but likes to feign indifference to the press.

"Why don't you drop some tidbits regarding the upcoming hearing? It wouldn't hurt to let him know I'm concerned about Pierson's corporate tax return and thinking of asking Treasury to look into the matter."

Not only is Trendle not looking into the company's finances, but he could care less. Financial scandals are never of interest to him.

"Sure."

With that, he's out the door. This is a classic red herring. Throw the oilmen off the scent and let them spin their wheels prepping for a financial assault that's never coming. "Josh, Mark here. You have time for a drink?"

"Today?"

"Yeah, this afternoon, I've got something you'll find interesting." He's always trolling for fresh news so I knew he couldn't resist. We meet at a small pub near Dupont Circle. After downing a couple of brews and chatting about inconsequential matters for a few minutes, Josh cuts to the chase. "Mark, you didn't call me to catch up on college football scores. What do you have?"

"This is from an unnamed source. Is that clear?"

He looks disappointed but knows me well enough not to violate the rules. "Sure, if you insist."

"The recent oil spill off New Jersey means the Energy Committee is scheduling a hearing."

He grunts, "That isn't news."

"No, but the fact that Trendle is considering asking Treasury to investigate Pierson Petroleum for an irregularity in their tax filing is."

"How real is this?"

"A highly placed staffer, who wishes to remain anonymous, overheard the congressman discussing the possibility."

"Come on, Mark. I can't go to print without verifying the info and seeking comments from Pierson Petroleum."

Josh suspects I'm using him. As a seasoned reporter, he's been used before and accepts it as part of the game he needs to play to stay connected to his sources.

"I understand."

Trendle knows this will never make the papers. But the fact that a Hill reporter contacts Pierson to confirm or deny the rumor will be enough to send them on a wild goose chase.

As we part ways, a thought pops into my head. "Josh, you ever get a call from a bill collector at five in the morning threatening your credit?" I ask with as much disinterest as possible.

"What happened, you max out your cards?"

"That's the odd part. I pay them off every month without fail. I tried finding the outfit on the web and it appears it doesn't exist."

"It's probably someone playing a joke on you."

"That thought crossed my mind, but when I contacted the credit rating agency, it appears someone was trying to steal my identity, which raised a flag on their system."

"What's the name of the outfit? I'll sniff around a bit and if I hear anything, I'll let you know. It's probably nothing, though."

FOUR

Our intent is to paint the oil companies, especially their executives, as mean and greedy in the hope that perverted logic convinces the public that the oil industry is preventing Americans from reaping the benefits of unchecked consumption and a carbon-free environment, all at the same time.

Trendle leaves the warm-up questions to other members of the committee. Albertson from Kentucky leads off. "Mr. Blankenphal, this committee would like to know precisely how this unfortunate accident occurred."

"Sir, we are working closely with the shipping company to try and understand the sequence of events."

"It's been a month since the spill. Surely, your experts must have found something."

"Congressman, to a layman such as yourself, it's difficult to explain the complexities involved."

That sets a few members grumbling about the arrogance of this guy.

Trendle retains his composure. Pushing his comb-over back in place, he steps in. "Thank you for enlightening us."

Blankenphal looks up sharply, no doubt suspicious of Trendle's sincerity. For the next forty-five minutes, the hearing drags on. Questions are asked and the Pierson team responds with lawyerly caution, supplying no real information.

"Mr. Blankenphal," says Trendle, suddenly breathing fire. "Tell this committee why eight years ago you shipped oil in *The Mistress of the Sea*, an unsafe, single-hull tanker you must have known failed numerous inspections." Leaving no time for Blankenphal to answer, Trendle continues, "And while you're at it, at least four other ships of yours were cited for safety violations during this same time period."

We then walk Blankenphal through every substandard safety report that the Coast Guard had on file for the last ten years. This is all a setup, as we know he can't possibly respond to the reports in any detail.

"Mr. Chairman, as you can imagine, I'm very concerned about safety, but we have to trust that the companies we lease ships from are sailing seaworthy vessels."

Letting the room fall silent, Trendle then asks in that quiet sort of way that rivets everyone's attention, "Mr. Blankenphal, can you tell this committee who the principal stockholder of Trans Petroleum Shipping is; the company you lease the ships from?"

Squirming in his seat, he replies, "Mr. Chairman, it's a publicly traded company for which its board of directors provides overall policy guidance."

"Mr. Blankenphal," Trendle fires back. "Who is the largest single stockholder of Trans Petroleum?"

Blankenphal's already ruddy complexion turns lobster-red. "As I said, it's publicly traded and there is no single majority stockholder of the company."

Trendle almost leaps over the dais and puts his hands around Blankenphal's neck. "Enough of this charade!" he shouts. "Public records show you own 27 percent of the company; and your wife, three sons, and sister each own 5 percent. It sounds to me like the Blankenphal family controls the company and should take personal responsibility for the oil spill. Furthermore, I want to know why the ship that contaminated the pristine waters off New Jersey's resort communities is still operating."

A few member of the committee start chuckling. Even I think Trendle is over the top at the mention of "pristine waters" and New Jersey in the same sentence. Blankenphal is at first dumbfounded and then makes the fatal mistake of answering without knowing the facts.

"I can assure you that Trans Petroleum has put the safety issues behind them, and their ships currently meet or exceed all federal requirements for seaworthiness."

"Then how do you explain the fact that the Coast Guard grounded this ship two years ago because the hull was showing signs of metal fatigue?" crowed Trendle. His voice quivers with righteous anger as the Coast Guard report he is waving about comes apart with pages flying every which way.

"The report specifically states the ship is not seaworthy. Why! Why! Why is it still sailing today?" yells Trendle, glasses falling off his nose.

FIVE

The hearing is a smashing success. The governors of New York and New Jersey pledge to redouble efforts to inspect ships suspected of safety violations. Senators from both states promise to sponsor legislation that adds a surcharge tax on the oil companies to pay for cleanup and to fund alternative sources of energy. The press is having a field day. The network news shows' experts are my personal favorite. "Pierson Petroleum should be made to pay; the EPA and Coast Guard are incompetent and renewable energy is the solution," says Professor Longworth, my adversary from a few weeks back. We listen to versions of this position from a score of environmental experts. Of course, the scapegoat petroleum-industry representative tries, with little success, to assure everyone that the spill wasn't really the oil industry's fault.

The drudgery comes after the fanfare is over. Alone in our conference room, I'm faced with thousands of pages of testimony that have to be sorted and cataloged. Leafing through mounds of white papers, briefs, and analyses, I come across a piece of written testimony that didn't make the hearing. I wouldn't have given it a second look except for the logo on the bottom, TCC International. That grabs my attention, as the firm and its CEO, Brig. Gen. T.C. Clarkson (retired) are major supporters of Trendle.

TCC International generates a regular supply of studies and position papers, and Clarkson himself often testifies at environmental Congressional hearings. Needless to say, Clarkson and the firm have become a self-perpetuating consulting engine. The more they publish and testify, the more the business community believes they can influence elected officials. The firm is clever and subtle. It never lobbies directly for earmarks, but sets up members of Congress with the appropriate guidance so the particular firm that TCC happens to represent at the time can send in its in-house lobbyist to close the deal.

When Clarkson is pontificating, usually in support of a business interest, his walking stick, the result of an old injury, becomes an extension of his arm, swinging wildly about as he makes a point. That point invariably comes around to telling all who will listen that the health of the environment and the health of the economy are two sides of the same coin. For all of Clarkson's visibility, however, he's a very private, even snobbish person. When hard or embarrassing questions come his way, he has the ability to respond at considerable length without revealing much, if anything, of substance. Several times when I've broached issues he's uncomfortable with, his wrath has descended upon me like the plague. And I learned, there's one area that's off-limits. During a recent conversation, I mentioned that *The New York Times* reported that Con-Gen is under investigation for refusing to bring overseas profits back to the states, thus evading US tax law.

His walking stick immediately went into motion. Pointing it directly at me, he shouted, "Mark, if you value your future, you better put a lid on that kind of talk. Accusing Con-Gen of criminal activity, when they are merely exercising their legitimate right to avoid unnecessary taxes, is libel in my book."

Clarkson's relationship with Con-Gen is such that he tolerates no criticism of the company for any reason. Thus, I'm shocked that the report, written by TCC International, I've just stumbled over is highly critical of the industries Clarkson supports. It accuses the oil industry of being in league with certain environmental firms and foreign bankers to manipulate financial markets. It lays out what seems like a far-fetched scheme to generate illegal profits by manipulating stakeholders at both ends of the spectrum: Big Oil and the environmental community. The author is none other than Connie Imlen, PhD. She must have submitted this directly without getting managements approval.

Imlen's dead, possibly murdered and now this. The next morning I bring the report to Trendle's attention. I see a hint of fear before his face freezes into a mask of feigned indifference.

"Mark, I'm sure this is from one of those right-wing radicals. Don't spend any time with it. I'll take care of it."

I thought that was it until the next day, when Trent Watersworth, Trendle's West Coast district office manager, calls. "Mark, how do you know Connie Imlen?"

"I don't, other than seeing her name on the report."

"Has she tried to meet with the congressman in person?"

Not wanting to share my own fears I simply said, "Trent, she stopped by earlier this month looking to meet with me regarding some issues,""

"Did she say what issues?"

"No, just that they were related to the environment."

"Are you sure?"

Annoyance is setting in. "Look, Trent, I told you all I know. Is there something you're not telling me?"

Suddenly he ends the call. "Not at all, forget you ever saw the paper. We'll take care of it."

I'm immediately suspicious regarding the "we" in who will take care of it. The twitch in my gut tells me there's something more behind this. Worse, I'm sure Trendle and Watersworth are hiding something. Despite their advice to forget, my curiosity is roused and I'm determined to find out what's behind the paper.

Two days later, hoping to be connected to a coworker, I call the main number at TCC International and ask for Connie Imlen. With hushed hesitancy, the receptionist replies, "I'm sorry; Ms. Imlen no longer works for the firm." Thinking quickly, I ask, "Can you connect me with her supervisor? I have flowers to deliver to her." Gambling that the receptionist doesn't know her personally, I add, "They appear to be for her birthday."

The voice on the other end of the line takes on a chill. "Ms. Imlen is no longer employed because she's deceased." Before I can ask what happened, she hangs up.

The Internet yields no additional information about her death. I decide to enlist some professional help and know just who to call. To ensure privacy, I slip into Trendle's office while he's at an industry-sponsored luncheon.

"Chet Southers, private investigator," a drowsy voice responds.

Southers is a private eye whom the House Finance Committee summoned to testify about a year and a half back. Chet himself wasn't under investigation. However, he did provide colorful insight into the intimate details of a powerful lobbyist's use of a DC escort service to show gratitude for services—or should I say legislation—rendered.

I still remember his testimony.

"Mr. Chairman, the congressman's wife hired me to find out who her husband was meeting with so late at night."

"What aroused her suspicion?"

"She had trouble understanding how he could be attending committee meetings when Congress was in recess." That drew a few chuckles from the audience. Southers knew how to work a crowd. His disarmingly laid-back style and lanky, slouched frame lent an air of disinterest, though his eyes told a different story. The intensity was unmistakable. "I caught him and the escort on camera in various intimate positions and showed the pictures to his wife. Since she paid the household bills, she had access to his cell phone records. After comparing the dates of his escort visits to his call log, I noticed the congressman always called the same number on those days."

"And whose number was it?" one of the committee members asked.

"The lobbyist in question." After a pause, he continued, "I guess his wife felt it was her patriotic duty to report this coincidence to your ethics office." More laughter erupted as Chet was excused.

Now, I tell Southers's receptionist, "I'd like to speak to Mr. Southers about a personal matter."

"We receive many requests of that nature," she responds. After a moment's pause, she continues, "Mr. Southers is in a meeting right now. Can I have him call you back?"

I'm not surprised he avoids direct calls; undoubtedly, many angry husbands call threatening to blow his brains out.

"Tell Chet this is Mark Burnham from Congressman Trendle's office. I'm calling in connection with the sworn testimony he gave before the congressional committee last year."

A note of caution creeps into the receptionist's voice. "Please hold a minute. I believe Mr. Southers conference has just ended." Nothing like the implied threat of congressional inquiry to free up someone's schedule.

"This is Chet Southers. What can I do for you?"

"Chet, I listened to your testimony last year regarding the lobbying scandal."

"And what is that good congressman they were investigating doing these days?" he asks.

"About five years in the federal penitentiary," I shoot back.

He grunts in the manner of someone who knows when to listen. "OK, Mark, you have my attention. What gives?"

"This is a personal matter. I need the services of an experienced PI."

"You're not engaged in some deep background investigation of escort services, are you?"

"Nothing so glamorous," I reply with a laugh. I brief him on the hearing and the paper Connie Imlen authored. I mention Trendle's reaction and the grilling by Watersworth. "Chet, it's probably all a coincidence, but the reaction of my boss and Imlen's suspicious death have me concerned."

"You want me to check out Trendle and Watersworth? That could get me in hot water if they ever find out."

"No, nothing like that. I'd just like to know about the circumstances of Imlen's death and any background about her that might shed some light on this."

"That I can do," he says, clearly relieved

"What do I owe you?"

"The initial research is on the house," Chet replies. "If you want something more after you hear what I have, we can talk price then."

I thank him and am about to hang up when he adds, "Mark, keep your eyes open and be careful. Make note of any unusual incidents you observe in the office. Your boss's reaction is evidence of something that could be illegal.

SIX

The Imlen incident has me reconsidering what that feisty professor dropped on my desk as he was leaving.

"Is Professor Longworth available? This is Mark Burnham from Congressman Trendle's office." I checked the professor's schedule and knew he was away on a lecture series. As I expected, the receptionist forwarded my call to one of his graduate students.

"This is Bernie. What do you want?" The attitude in this guy's voice tells me he was one of the three students who accompanied the professor to our meeting.

I need a hook to pique his curiosity. "Bernie, listen, I just stumbled upon some news the professor will find very interesting. When can you stop over?"

This catches him off guard. "I think you'd better discuss whatever it is with Professor Longworth," he replies cautiously.

"It's too hot to wait and involves that news article your boss dropped on me regarding the murder of an environmental whistleblower."

He's even more suspicious when I ask him to meet me at my apartment that night, but curiosity gets the best of him and he finally agrees.

"Great. See you at ten."

SEVEN

Few outside Congress realize that during the weeks leading up to Earth Day, an annual spring assault on every member of Congress by well-intentioned, though not always well-informed environmental activists takes place. Joining them are the political wannabes and lobbyists primed to profit from the greening of the budget.

What's truly alarming is the amount of money being thrown at politicians for self-serving reasons that have little to do with the environment. Genuine progress is too easily derailed by the allure of wealth and fear of powerful enemies. Admittedly, in a small corner of my conscious resides a nagging concern that even Congressman Trendle, the noblest champion of a carbon-free environment, is at risk of being corrupted by his supporters who regularly throw lots of money his way. I'm ever vigilant in protecting his reputation and keeping a finger on the pulse of the vast environmental conversation flowing through the electronic media.

While deeply passionate about the environment, I've always preferred the hard-nosed intellectual debate. To this day, I remember my high school biology teacher, Mr. Newhouse, verbally beating my skinny, acne-decorated attitude into the floorboards by questioning my impassioned speech about saving the environment.

"Facts, facts, and more facts, young man!" Mr. Newhouse said, glaring at me. "Emotion is like fireworks on the Fourth of July. They look great but fade fast. Its facts supported by hard research that make the real difference. If you're not in it for the long haul, than it's not really passion," he spit out. "It's just a fad."

With that, he went back to whatever he was teaching that day. But I never forgot it and from that point on, I mastered the details of whatever position I supported, developed a bulldog persistence in defending it and the discipline to stay on topic until I've bested the opposition.

It was four years ago that Trendle gave me my big break. "Mark, can you come into my office? There's something I want to discuss with you." Coming around from his desk and sitting in a chair next to the sofa where I was perched, he said, "Melanie has just resigned and I'd like you to replace her as my chief of staff."

I was stunned, not only at the surprise announcement of Melanie's departure but that Trendle would promote me ahead of others with more seniority. "Congressman, those are big shoes to fill. Are you sure I'm ready?"

"You are the hardest-working team member I have, but that's not the only reason. It's because you demand legitimate research, seek real information, and will challenge even our environmental allies—and me—if you disagree with a position. I don't need yes men. There're a dime a dozen."

I continued to question my readiness when he raised his hand to stop me. "Answer me this. Why do you think the work we are engaged in is so important?"

I thought for a moment and then spoke from the heart. "Americans fight over every conceivable issue, ranging from taxes to the global war on terrorism. But it's the looming environmental meltdown that tops all of them. What good is fixing the tax code if we can no longer breathe the air? Why fight terrorism if we're left with a planet unable to sustain itself?"

With a smile and handshake, Trendle said, "Congratulations, Mark, the job is yours for the reasons I've already given and because you get what this is really about."

"Wealthy donors of Trendle are in bed with one of America's biggest contributors to carbon pollution: Con-Gen Industries. They will stop at nothing, including murder, to achieve their goals, for generations, their connection with the Preston family has ensured that the interests of countries in the Western hemisphere are subverted by their lust for power and unchecked greed!"

Con-Gen is a traditional manufacturer that has seen the environmental light. Sure, it still produces carbon, but change takes time. And the Prestons are wealthy, doddering spinsters of no account other than they support Trendle. My usual reaction is: "Where do bloggers dream up this stuff?"

With Connie Imlen's death, I'm no longer sure.

Just then, my cell rings. "Mark, it's Josh. We need to talk."

"What's up?"

"Remember when you asked me about the call from the collection agency?"

"Yeah."

"We should meet. It's not something I can tell you over the phone. Meet me at five at our usual hangout."

I'm feeling weak in the knees. What in God's name is going on? My mouth's suddenly gone dry and the knot in my gut has returned. Josh is not one to exaggerate. This must be serious and he's worried. The fact that he specifically mentioned "hangout" told me we were staying away from the regular congressional watering holes and meeting at the bar down the street from the ball field where we play in a summer softball league.

"Josh, what's up? You have me nervous."

He motions for me to be quiet and leads me to the far end of the bar, which is empty at this hour. "Mark, I managed to track down where that early morning call came from."

"How the hell did you do that?"

"I have friends in low places at your wireless carrier." He looks around nervously before continuing. "What is your connection to the Wind Research Institute?"

My mind starts racing. "Josh, that's in the heart of Trendle's district. The institute is his baby and is backed by his most influential supporters. Could you tell whose phone it came from?"

"It looks like it came from a bank of phones assigned to the Institute rather than a particular individual."

It had to be the phones that volunteers use to reach out and raise funds.

With his hand poised as if holding a gun he says, "Someone has you in their sights."

We talk for another thirty minutes. In spite of the fear, anger is my predominant emotion and I'm determined to get to the bottom of this.

As I head to the Metro, I'm thinking about Clarkson's reaction when I mentioned *The New York Times* article suggesting Con-Gen is guilty of tax evasion. That, along with the grilling that Watersworth laid on me regarding the Imlen report, has to have been the trigger. They're suspicious and this may be their way of scaring me.

There is someone who may know the answer. At home, I rummage through my desk and find her number.

"Is this Melanie?"

I passed on my suspicions to Chet, and he tracked down the phone number of Melanie Donovan. She was Trendle's chief of staff whose sudden departure resulted in my promotion to the position.

"Yes," she says with a note of caution in her voice.

"This is Mark Burnham." It takes her a few moments to recall who I am.

"Oh, yes. I heard that you replaced me as chief of staff. Are you still on the job?"

"Why wouldn't I be?"

"Oh, no reason, what can I do for you?" she says, quickly composing herself.

"I never had a chance to talk with you before you left." I decide there was little sense in beating around the bush. "Were you forced out?"

I hear her breathing quicken but she says nothing. After a long silence, she finally says, "I'm sorry. There's nothing I can tell you."

I can hear it in her voice. "What are you afraid of?"

"When I resigned, I agreed not to disclose the reasons."

Before I can speak, she hangs up.

She's obviously hiding something and I'm inclined to believe there was some kind of formal separation agreement, which means she was paid off.

I bolt out the door of my apartment, jump into the car, and head south toward Quantico. Melanie's address is in the town of Stafford, south of the Marine base. It's just after eight when I knock on the door. It takes about a minute before a middle-aged man greets me. Judging by his haircut, demeanor, and obvious fitness, he has to be a Marine. "What can I do for you?" he says with considerable suspicion.

The moment I mention my name, he steps outside, closes the door behind him, and grabs both my shoulders with painful force. "Son, Melanie told me you called. She made it clear she didn't want to speak with you and now I'm telling you to back off and don't bother us again." With that, he enters the house and slams the door in my face.

Driving back to DC, two thoughts occur to me: This is deeper than I thought and I'm pretty sure somebody is following me. I didn't give much thought to the gray Explorer that passed as I pulled over in front of Melanie's house, but now I'm sure it's the same vehicle that's several cars behind me as I return to DC. After crossing into the District, I lose of track of it.

EIGHT

I make it back to my apartment with ten minutes to spare. Bernie, Longworth's grad student, should be here any minute. I pop open a couple of beers just as my doorbell buzzes. I let Bernie in and hand him a beer.

"Thanks for stopping by. That article you left on my desk was right on."

He's unsettled and I don't want to give him time to put up defenses.

"How well did your Professor know Connie Imlen?"

"Not at all," Bernie responds.

Hoping to peak his curiosity I tell him about the paper that she authored.

He is about to ask me something when caution gets the best of him.

He abruptly ends the conversation. "I really shouldn't be talking to you."

"Let's keep in touch. If I hear anything more, I'll give you a call on your cell?" I tell him.

I expect Bernie will tell Longworth about our meeting. He may encourage Bernie to work with me in hopes that I'll become another source of information they can use.

NINE

Trendle has an uncanny ability to compromise over tactics without surrendering principle. It's a skill shared by all successful politicians and it's what makes this city work. What tourists wandering the streets of DC see is something of an illusion. The granite edifices and stately buildings project a sense of order, purpose, and simplicity that doesn't exist. It's the thrust and parry of powerful politicians and their minions, I being one of them, which defines Washington. It's because of political accommodations that Trendle cuts the coal industry a break.

One of Trendle's political consultants has stopped by the office to discuss fund-raising strategy. Glenn Malvern has engineered the successful reelection of scores of politicians. While waiting for Trendle, he and I fall into conversation around the whole coal issue.

"Glenn, I can't understand how coal manages to fly under much of the environmental scrutiny, including our own."

He smiles, sitting back in the chair. "You've heard the term 'strange bedfellows'?"

"Sure, but the environmental polar opposites in West Virginia are unbelievable. I know the governor and Trendle are longtime friends but—"

Before I can complete the thought, he interrupts, "Not so. Let me explain. Coal has achieved this remarkable lack of attention because, as is often the case, disparate interests coalesce in support of a common cause."

"But what can possibly be the common cause?" I challenge.

"Mark, you're forgetting the most basic tenet of a good compromise: Everybody wins. The strategy I'm here to discuss with your boss is brilliant. First, the mining companies dynamite a range of hills filled with coal, excavating millions of tons of black gold. These same companies then rebuild the scarred landscape into gently rolling hills and meadows. The unions love the construction jobs this brings to the region. A generous donation to the Blue Sky Club ensures that trees are planted and bike and hiking paths are built to transform once uninspired land into a magnet for outdoor enthusiasts. The hunters support this because it attracts game, which inevitably wander onto property owned by the local gun club. To the uninitiated, it seems the land must have been that way from the beginning."

"OK, I get that. But how does that satisfy the foes of carbon?"

"Well, that's where this gets really interesting. The best part of the West Virginia miracle is that the state legislature insists that constant-speed wind turbines must be erected at the coal sites. It makes a lot of sense to the power companies, as the biggest drawback to wind is its unreliability. The method that overcomes this deficiency is both technologically and politically attractive. By combining each windmill with another power source, the wind turbines maintain a constant speed of rotation twenty-four/seven. When the wind is sufficiently strong, it is the sole source of power. The remaining time, the alternative power source kicks in, supplementing the wind, ensuring that a steady supply of electricity is produced. The power companies gain access to tax-subsidized electricity. The "Greens," though reluctant at first, ultimately throw their support behind the technology once they realize this is the best they can hope for. Since the supplemental source of power is fueled by coal gas, the mining companies and the unions are enthusiastic. Finally, the Coal Producers' Association runs endless ads stating that clean coal technology is the natural partner in building America's renewable energy future. It's the same reason the Association seldom complains about ethanol. After all, tons of coal is needed to cook the corn mash in preparation for the fermentation process. While ethanol is good for coal, it's a lousy solution—other than keeping Iowa farmers happy."

My contribution to building this partnership is gaining the support of Congressman Cletus from Kansas for the latest expansion of wind power. While he could care less about West Virginia, his vote on the Energy Committee is critical to making it happen. Every legislator's style is different. When Trendle needs me to connect on a specific issue, he doesn't make the request directly.

After the rest of the staff goes home for the night, Trendle pops into my office.

"Mark, that bastard Cletus is a real pain in my ass about the funding we need to continue the expansion in West Virginia," he says at the top of his lungs. "If I hear one more complaint about the lack of sufficient farm subsidy for those wealthy corporate farmers, I'm tempted to call a press conference just to embarrass him." He turns to leave the room, but not before adding, "And let me tell you, I'm not about doing favors for that one. Just let him try me."

Trendle knows this is one of those occasions when the favor is needed from a member of the House whose support is vital in moving the bill from committee to a floor vote. As I'm digesting Trendle's rant, the phone rings. It's Chet Southers with the information I requested.

Apparently, Connie Imlen, actually Professor Imlen, was one of the foremost authorities on nuclear power-plant accidents in her early years. She and her husband, Conrad Imlen, fresh out of Stamford University's doctoral program on particle physics, coauthored a paper that identified a number of critical weaknesses in the design of early nuclear reactors. The industry was up in arms, which, as it turned out, backfired because the Imlens' paper came to the attention of President Kennedy's director of the Department of Energy, who was responsible for the scant nuclear power safety regulation in existence at the time. The director invited the Imlens to join the department and lead the effort to create comprehensive regulatory language. Connie's husband declined the offer and remained a university researcher, but she embraced the challenge. She also served as an investigator who was sent to analyze all significant incidents at power plants.

"She was quite the rising star back then. Professor Imlen led the Department of Energy's investigation of the partial meltdown of the Enrico Fermi-1 Fast Breeder reactor back in the sixties. It was located thirty miles from Detroit on the shores of Lake Erie," says Southers.

"If she was such star, why haven't we heard of her in the committee?"

"That's just it. All of a sudden, she dropped off the radar and refused any further interviews."

"Were you able to find out why?"

"Nothing from any of my sources, but it occurred right after she gave an interview in which she blasted the engineers who designed the reactor's coolant system as morons."

That kind of colorful language was bit unusual coming from a government bureaucrat.

"Did the article indicate why she thought this?"

"Yeah, it quoted her at length regarding the sheer madness of using liquid sodium, one of nature's most unstable elements, to cool the reactor's core. It was her judgment that if the coolant itself had leaked and been exposed to air or water, the entire plant would have been destroyed by the resulting explosion and fire. According to her scenario, the Fermi accident would have made Chernobyl look like child's play."

"That sounds pretty serious. What happened to Connie between then and now?"

"She held several university posts and a couple of industry positions. Apparently, the Fermi incident and accompanying politics associated with nuclear power, along with her being blackballed by the Department of Energy, soured her against nuclear power. She remade herself as a specialist in renewable energy and was serving as an analyst for TCC International at the time of her death."

Southers finishes up and I thank him for the information. He promises to send over a copy of the local police report regarding the nature of her accidental death.

I'm about to hang up when he adds, "Mark, that other item you faxed over..." I'd completely forgotten I'd sent over what I knew about Melanie's abrupt departure as chief of staff and her tough-looking husband.

The tone of his voice tells me it's not good news.

"The day after you visited the Donovans, Melanie's husband was transferred to the Marine division stationed in Okinawa."

"When are they leaving?"

"They're gone. In one day, the Marines moved the entire family. The house is empty and already up for sale."

I'm stunned.

"Mark, you still there?"

"Yeah, I'm here."

"Whatever's going on, you certainly seem to have stirred up a hornet's nest. I'd be careful if I were you."

As we hang up, Shauna walks into my office. With a sheepish expression, she asks, "Mark, who were you talking to on the phone?" Seeing the look on my face she quickly adds, "I'm so sorry, but the congressman has ordered me to keep a log of every call coming in and out of the office."

"This is outrageous. I'll take this up with Trendle."

"Please don't," she simpers. "The congressman told me that the Speaker of the House ordered all committee heads to institute this practice because of recent allegations being looked at by the ethics committee."

This, I hadn't heard.

"Mark, I'm only following orders."

I decide to keep quiet and ask my counterparts if they've heard about such an order. This is entirely too coincidental coming after the discovery of Imlen's report, her unexplained death, and Melanie's abrupt departure. My suspicions and uneasiness are now on overdrive. And making the call to Southers from Trendle's office was a mistake, as he's obviously checking all calls. The knot in my stomach creeps back.

Meanwhile, the pace of activity is heating up, keeping me from checking this out right away. Trendle's threat of a press conference is a bogey. He very rarely calls one to attack a colleague. I've seen it done twice in seven years. One of them was directed at a fellow Democrat who was not sufficiently supportive of an important energy bill that Trendle was sponsoring. In both cases, the press conferences were so well orchestrated and devastating to the political careers of the targeted individuals that members live in fear of Trendle's wrath going public. I've learned that a weapon that powerful is best when it is not used, only implied.

Secondly, Trendle's remark about not doing favors is a coded message for me to connect with Cletus's staff and begin the horse-trading in earnest. Bev McCann, Cletus's chief of staff, attends the same monthly energy-industry forum I do. It's sponsored by the Council for Clean Coal and just happens to be this evening. It will be easy enough to connect with her there.

"Hey Bev," I say when I spot her at the forum. "We'd love to find a way to throw up another seventy-five windmills in West Virginia."

She laughs as one does with a friend, which we are. "Over Cletus's dead body, why would he care, anyway?" she says. When I don't respond, she looks up to see my expressionless face and gives me a barely perceptible nod.

Nothing more needs to be said. The opening salvoes have been fired. Let the games begin.

Two days after Bev and I connected, Cletus's office distributes a white paper on the challenges of creating manufacturing jobs in the US. Naturally, it highlights his district as the ideal location for new blue-collar jobs. The truth is that Cletus advocates so successfully, unemployment in his district is well below the national average. But that's beside the point. His goal is to maintain a track record of success that ensures perpetual reelection. While the paper was delivered to the in-basket of every member of Congress, only our copy had a handwritten note at the bottom: "Great opportunity to put Americans to work." That told us all we needed to know. If we can find a way to put renewable energy jobs in Cletus's district, he'll support us.

That afternoon, I'm on a flight to the West Coast for an ad hoc meeting with the most important members of the WW9: T. C. Clarkson, Lydia (Liddy) Van Flugete, self made millionaire Malcolm Little and the Rumple Sisters, .

The Sisters are Betty, Jane, and Miranda. While their real last name is Preston, they are universally known, behind their backs, of course, as the Rumple Sisters. This is as much a result of the pre-war (I'm talking WWI) clothing they wear as it is a testament to their eccentric personalities. Apparently, wrinkle-free clothing is not a priority for them as they consistently wear peasant dresses that could have been on the Donner expedition. They are lifelong spinsters, all well north of eighty in age. The sisters are beneficiaries of "old money" that has its origins in the great California and Alaska gold rushes. Old man Preston knew that the real treasure lay in transporting the endless hoards of fools searching for gold. They booked passage on his ships, bought supplies from his stores, and, according to legend, partook of the delights offered by his traveling "seamstresses."

Most of the time, the Rumple Sisters chatter about the weather, what's on sale at Wal-Mart and a host of other inconsequential things in that random way people do with those they've known all their lives. But mention money, especially if it involves theirs, and suddenly they're totally focused. They want to know every detail of any request for a donation, whether charitable or political, showing more zeal than the FBI probing a money-laundering operation. Truth be told, they are so miserly that they are among the tightest of the wealthy donors. But the sisters' very quirkiness assures that the local press frequently features them as patrons of Trendle, which more than compensates for the diminutive size of their contributions.

We talk in Liddy's dining room, which has a magnificent view of the Pacific.

"Let me show you my latest creation!" says an excited Little.

As he often does, Little opens gatherings by introducing a new, usually weird, painting or sculpture that we naturally fawn over. He feels the need to demonstrate continuously that he is the premier artist of the human form. We gush over a naked Lady Godiva sitting on a three-legged horse, though we never do find out the point of the missing leg.

"Mark," purrs Liddy, "glad you could join us for dinner. What's new in Washington?"

It all sounds so casual with Liddy strutting about, Sea Breeze in hand and draped in a designer kaftan atop stilettos. It's an unusual combo but with her beauty and build, it works. A fly on the wall would have thought we just happened to show up at the same place and time to admire art and gossip—that it was somehow a happy coincidence.

"Congressman Trendle sends his regards and wants you to know he is fighting hard to have the Great Pacific Meadow declared a national arboretum. He has Bell from Michigan and Stuyvescent of New Mexico on board," I tell them.

This is the eternal pipe-dream project that's music to their ears. Trendle knows this is a task worthy of Don Quixote. However, it serves its purpose as the red herring he needs to bolster his supporters. It's a project that will never happen. I know it and Trendle knows it. No way is Congress going to set aside ten thousand acres of prime commercial real estate simply to protect a few wealthy tree huggers' backyard views. But since Liddy, Malcolm, and the Rumple Sisters love the idea, we raise the banner just as often as the lobbyist for the coalition of builders and Realtors knocks it down.

All the while, T.C. Clarkson sits unmoved and clearly uninspired by the collective joy over Malcolm's art and preservation of the view. Brig. Gen. (retired) T.C. Clarkson is invariably in attendance at WW9 gatherings. He's somewhat taller than average, a cadaverous individual radiating the warmth of dead mackerel.

"Mark, what does Tom want?" he finally interrupts. I knew this was coming and I'm prepared.

"General, he sees an unbelievable opportunity to reduce the carbon footprint in West Virginia and Kansas while at the same time expanding jobs by supporting our domestic industrial base." I remind them of the constant-speed windmills in West Virginia and the small windmill farm in Kansas. I paint a pastoral vision of the windmills lovingly spinning in the gentle breeze that flows across the plains of Kansas right through the middle of Cletus's district. Never mind the tornados that threaten and occasionally demolish some of them. The sisters are leaning forward in their chairs with excitement. Liddy shoots me that knowing look along with her great smile.

Did I mention that it seems Liddy feels the two of us should have more quality time together? The image of a cougar flashes in my head. I can't deny that she is incredibly attractive and could definitely provide a pleasant distraction. But Liddy is like the jelly doughnut that tastes great going down but will burn a hole in your stomach for the rest of the day. That kind of heartburn I don't need, and so far, I've managed to avoid such an entanglement without offending her.

Liddy is a woman of many charms and significant connections. She loves to dabble in matchmaking for both herself and others, and there always seems to be enough young, attractive women at her parties to join the males in attendance. In fact, after attending a few such events, I got to know the regulars, who all exhibit a special loyalty to Liddy. The truth is, I probably do need a woman in my life, but with my zest for politics and a reputation for single-mindedness, I either need to find someone completely uninterested in politics, which does not particularly appeal to me, or connect with a woman who shares my passion for the power of good government. Such a woman is not Liddy.

The absurdity of it all is that the number of windmills we're considering, spinning at one hundred miles an hour day and night, will barely generate enough power to heat the WW9s' collection of Olympic-size pools. Malcolm predictably asks a few questions about the need for private financing and the potential to attract international investors. The sisters, hearing money mentioned, look ready to put on the green eyeshades. The discussion continues for a few minutes with Malcolm waxing eloquent about international reinsurance, Caspian Sea investors, and Swiss banking support.

Clarkson finally has enough.

"Here's how I see it. A large industrial corporation—read Con-Gen—would have trouble getting excited about this. While the West Virginia program has sufficient scale, the Kansas wind farm is hardly worth any Fortune 100's time. The energy producers know that if wind is ever to be a significant contributor in feeding the nation's grid, then new, long-range transmission lines have to be erected and the existing system overhauled."

Con-Gen is not an energy producer, but I knew where this was going. Transmission systems translate to steel for towers, copper wire, manufacturing, and assembly, all right up Con-Gen's alley.

Two days later, I brief Trendle, alone of course, and the deal is struck. Con-Gen happens to propose, via its lobbyist, building state-of-the-art windmills in Kansas on several wheat fields adjacent to the current wind farm. They plan is to refurbish an abandoned factory in Cletus's district, where component parts made in Mexico will be assembled. The NAFTA proponents love it, and eighty-five new jobs get Cletus his press conference. Con-Gen receives quiet assurance that Trendle and Cletus will direct renewable-energy money to them for transmission-line upgrades.

Most importantly, Cletus is suddenly an avid cheerleader for the growth of wind power in West Virginia. Trendle waves this latest environmental green flag in front of a grateful WW9, the members of which line his campaign pockets with renewed enthusiasm.

As a byproduct, these wealthy Pacific Coasters love the fact that the ugly windmills are out of sight, thousands of miles away. And by the time any new transmission lines reach their neighborhood, they'll be buried underground. Best of all, it keeps Liddy and Malcolm busy hosting fund-raisers to add yet another exhibit to the Wind Research Institute, conveniently located in Trendle's district, proudly proclaiming that the congressman continues to lead the way in remaking America.

Everyone is happy except me. I'm convinced that I've acquired a shadow. After working my magic with Bev three days ago, I suspected someone was tailing me as I walked the six blocks from the Council for Clean Coal meeting to Capitol Hill. I wouldn't have noticed except that the undistinguished man stood out precisely because he appeared to be just out for a stroll. No one in DC is ever out for a stroll, especially around Capitol Hill. Pedestrians are either tourists or busy people marching purposefully to their next appointment to seek a favor from someone in power.

Just to check, I took a detour, stopping suddenly to put my cell phone to my ear and pretend to engage in an animated conversation. I cursed to myself as if I'd just been summoned and changed directions, heading back to our offices. He trailed me until I entered the building. I'd detected no one following me on the West Coast, but back in DC, an individual, not always the same one, was a hundred feet behind me wherever I went.

While pondering this latest development, my suspicions about Connie Imlen's death are confirmed as I scan a police report Chet sent over. Apparently, her death initially was ruled suspicious, as the investigator was unable to explain the break in the propane feeder line to the kitchen stove. It was pure luck that the apartment didn't explode. The building manager noticed a strong odor of gas coming from the apartment and promptly called the propane company. They, along with police and the fire department, managed to shut the gas off from the outside and carefully break open a couple of windows to ventilate the apartment. Connie Imlen was already dead and her elderly husband unconscious and barely breathing. He died three days later. Eventually officials ruled it an accident, concluding that Connie must have moved the stove to clean and inadvertently fractured the propane line.

I also checked in with a couple of staffers regarding the new phone log order. I casually mention that I'd heard a rumor this was coming down, but none of them are aware of it.

Since my suspicions are now confirmed, I call Southers's office from a pay phone after hours and leave him a voice message about the phone monitoring and people following me. I tell him not to call me at my office or on my cell. Instead, I'll reach out to him. On one level, I'm hurt that Trendle doesn't trust me. At a deeper level, I'm fearful that this is only the tip of a very big iceberg.

TEN

For Trendle, brokering deals and supporting the Wind Research Institute serve as a stepping-stone to achieving victory in the war over carbon. For all the pomp and noise he brings to bear, Trendle's no fool. He always keeps his eye on the long view. Early in my tenure, as a junior staffer, I was on my high horse complaining long and loud about the stupidity of the American people when it comes to oil. Trendle silenced me with a raised hand and said, "Mark, learn to be patient and claim victory for each step forward. After all, the chosen people spent four hundred years enslaved in Egypt and another forty wandering through the desert before they reached the Promised Land."

As a result of the success of the Jersey spill hearing we are one step closer. Trendle is the keynote speaker at five major environmental and alternative-energy functions over the next few weeks. He's welcomed with thunderous applause at all of them. Shauna, Kevin (our newest staff intern) and I make up Trendle's support team at these events. Shauna and Kevin take notes as Trendle presents, paying special attention to the question-and-answer segment. My job is to network with key donors and persons of influence while basking in the reflective glow of his success. Each evening, we debrief the day and identify what was asked and, more importantly, who asked the questions to identify potential reelection issues.

Still looking over my shoulder I carefully scan the crowds at each event for someone that might be keeping watch on me. So far, it seems I'm not on surveillance once I'm inside a function.

Toward the end of the event, sponsored by GreenFire, an offshoot environmental group funded largely by a billionaire liberal, I bump into the beaten-down apologist sent by the oil association.

"Hey Teddy," I call out as he walks by. "You took a few lumps from the audience this evening." Theodore Edelstein is a bookish scientist who is comfortable with facts but, as was obvious this evening, not with the shrill heckling of the opposition.

He stops and with a weary shake of his head says, "Sometimes I wonder why I ever left the EPA to join the Oil Association." That catches my attention.

"I didn't know you were with EPA. Why did you leave the pristine world of environmental purity for the much maligned oil industry?"

With a big sigh Teddy answers, "Listen, I need a drink. If you're really interested, join me."

I think about it for a minute and figure why not. Maybe I can pick up more ammo to use against the oil industry. We find a table in the hotel steak house and order our favorite poisons, scotch for me and a martini for Teddy. With that, he starts to unload.

"Leaving the EPA was the hardest career decision I ever made. I loved the environmental work and really do want to live in a cleaner world free from global warming"

"Of all the places you could have gone, why Big Oil?" I interrupt.

Teddy sips his drink, stares at the table for a moment, and then looks me in the eye. "Your boss's reputation is well known. Is this conversation going straight from my mouth to his ears?"

"It's true we have a bull's eye smack on top of the oil industry. But that doesn't mean I don't listen." The implication that I can't be trusted ticks me off. Somewhat heatedly, I add, "If you tell me this is just between the two of us, it will go no farther." After a moment, he nods. What unfolds is fascinating in its implications even if I have trouble digesting it.

"I started at the EPA fresh out of grad school with a master's in geology. The Clinton administration wanted the agency to broaden its expertise beyond marine biologists and chemists to include experts such as myself who understood and could decode what the oil industry is all about."

Makes sense to me, I think.

"And for the first ten years, I was deeply involved in analyzing every industry report that defended the burning of fossil fuel and the need for oil. Some of the arguments were disingenuous in disguising the damaging effects of drilling. But for the most part, they were relatively straightforward white papers that looked across a wide range of factors contributing to global warming. My job was to pull talking points from these papers, offer explanations as to some of the more esoteric oil terminology, and provide rebuttal language that the politicos would weave into congressional testimony. The other aspect of the work was reviewing how well the industry adhered to the many regulations designed to minimize compromise to the environment."

He stops to catch his breath and orders another drink. After refreshing my own, I remark, "I get all that, but it would seem to me that after ten years of this work, your blood would boil at the mere mention of oil."

"That's what everybody thinks, but just the opposite happened," he says, shaking his head. "What I began to realize is that for a lot of EPA disciples, the environment is their religion. Their zeal for all things clean and green blocks the ability of the agency to look at the bigger picture and ask itself what is real and what is bias? And most importantly, what is the truth?"

It seems obvious to me that EPA staffers should feel strongly about this, as I do. And I say so.

"Ah, but it's not that simple for three important reasons. First, the industry is often looked at in the same way as tobacco. Cigarette makers essentially have a vertical business model that locks in the growers, cures the tobacco, processes and makes the cigarettes, packages and delivers them to retailers, and promotes their use. Oil companies, on the other hand, drill and, in some cases, refine the crude into distillates. But that's where it ends. Thousands of other businesses, independent of the producers, buy the products for all sorts of uses ranging from cars to the chemical industry to electric power generation."

I can see his point but not the relevance. "So what, like tobacco, they have taken a product of nature and created an environmental monster?"

"And that leads me to the second reason. Oil, unlike tobacco, is not something that even in its heyday only a minority of the population used. There was and is the ability to walk away from smoking, personally and politically. The tobacco industry has a long history of promoting smoking to increase business, but that's not the case with oil. Independent companies, power generation, the military, advances in transportation—auto, rail, and air—all have made demands on oil that have fueled exploration. That doesn't mean billions aren't made by Big Oil wildcatters and speculators. They are. The point is that outside interest has driven the demand, not the oil industry. On top of this, it's not just one or two industries, but virtually every single one, and, with few exceptions, every citizen that wants the benefits derived from oil."

I start to protest but he challenges me.

"Mark, take out a pen and paper and make a list of everything in your congressional office that is derived from oil. As you prepare to attack the industry at the next hearing, think about all the physical items, the electronics, and the controlled environment you work in that exist because of oil."

I start making a mental list and quickly realize it's virtually everything.

"I'll concede your point, but shouldn't that be the incentive for working even harder to tear them down?"

"It might be, but you haven't heard the most compelling reason why oil is so tough to move away from."

I expect some global economics argument and I'm surprised when he simply says, "Oil is incredibly expansive." After noticing the confused look on my face, he apologizes. "I forget that it's not common knowledge among lay people that the more oil is processed, the more you get."

"What do you mean?"

"One barrel, forty-two gallons, of crude produces over forty-four gallons of distilled product." He sees the look of incredulity on my face. "It's true and that's why oil is so economically attractive. It is truly the wonder fuel and the most versatile of chemical raw materials all rolled into one."

In his own unassuming way, this guy is a master at defending what he believes in. He might not win the prize for showmanship, but Teddy is a keen thinker who knows how to organize and defend a particular position. As much as I want to yell at him, his arguments and quiet passion are engaging and persuasive.

"Gentlemen," the server interrupts, "how about some dinner?"

"Teddy, it's on me." I didn't want the discussion to end. It's the kind of one-on-one debate in which I love to engage. We both order rib-eye steaks and baked potatoes the size of nuclear submarines, figuring the meal will absorb the alcohol lubricating our discussion.

After dinner, we order another round of drinks. Judging it's my turn to bring the discussion back to the core problem, I launch into an impassioned monologue on the impact of global warming. "While I'll concede what you say has merit, it doesn't solve the problem brought on by the burning of fossil fuel. Scientists agree that the rise in mean global temperature over the last one hundred years closely tracks the growth in carbon dioxide released into the atmosphere as oil-based industrialization has mushroomed."

I take him through well-known arguments using Al Gore's *Inconvenient Truth* as a starting point. Teddy listens politely, asks a few clarifying questions, and jots some notes on a napkin as I preach the 'green' message. Feeling the flush of alcohol-stoked blood rush to my face, with finger pointed I conclude a little louder then intended. "The point is, regardless of how wonderful oil might be, it's killing the planet."

Satisfied that I had made my point, I sit back with an air of one who knows he's won the argument. Or so I think.

Teddy sits quietly for a few minutes, nods to himself a couple of times, and finally looks up. "The real reason I left the EPA was the lack of hope among the environmentalists and various affiliated green organizations that are leading the fight to clean up the environment. There's too much talk about population control and gloom-and-doom prophesies of the imminent death of the planet." He continues, moving his hands across an imaginary line in the sand. "True, the oil industry is filled with hard-nosed businessmen, greedy investors, and a host of short-sighted objectives, but the industry is one that is built on hope—that wonderful optimism that has energized this country for over two hundred years and given us the uncanny ability to see a bright future on the other side of whatever challenges we face, along with the will to overcome those challenges."

I interrupt, "But surely the incredible damage brought on by the burning of fossil fuel must be halted in its tracks."

"Mark, let me tell you a story."

I lean forward eagerly. In the couple of hours that we've been talking, a relationship and even the beginnings of a friendship have developed.

"In the nineteenth century, an event occurred in London known as The Great Stink. Prior to that, there had been a great deal of dialogue and public debate regarding the lack of proper sewage and the periodic outbreak of cholera," Teddy begins.

He is fully engaged. His hands are smoothly supplementing a voice that has taken on the richness of a thespian proclaiming Hamlet. Its all the more surprising coming from this diminutive geologist dressed conservatively in a button-down shirt and tie. Now he really has my attention. I want to know the ending to this story.

"In 1858, the combination of an ever-growing population and heavy, languishing weather caused an eruption of a stench so foul that even Parliament was preparing to flee

London. As you can imagine, there were all sorts of ideas for solutions floating around; everything from evacuating London and returning to an agrarian society to housing pigs in every neighborhood to consume the sewage."

Contemplating the last scenario takes the luster off the meal I'd just consumed.

He continues, seeing that I'm drawn into the story. "Adding to the crisis was a complete misunderstanding of the cause of cholera. Virtually every expert, with one notable exception, thought it was the result of breathing in the stink, which made sense. The more things stunk, the more outbreaks of cholera took place."

I'm beginning to see where he's going: obvious conclusions of cause and effect even among the so-called "enlightened" can and often are misleading or downright wrong. That reminds me of my own mantra: facts, facts, and more facts.

Teddy pauses to ask if I'm bored. "Not at all, please go on," I say, though I'm not quite ready to admit he may have a point.

"As with all change, it often only occurs as a result of crisis. And so it was with this environmental catastrophe. Two events happened. Parliament authorized the necessary funds to construct the first sewer system. It's still considered one of the modern marvels of engineering. It literally breathed new life and prosperity into London. The second was the diligent research and critical thinking a London physician brought to bear on the cholera problem. His research and perseverance revealed the true cause of the spread of the disease: unclean water, not smelly air, is at the root of the problem." He wraps up the story with a dramatic statement. "This seemingly local problem literally transformed human society because it was addressed, not by depressing rhetoric, but by hope-filled optimism that the human spirit and ingenuity would triumph."

My guess is that Teddy seldom finds a sympathetic ear that will take the time to listen. That resonated with me. While my love of politics is genuine, one of the drawbacks is there is little real dialogue. It's too often one group talking at another with neither side willing to listen.

"I see your point, but isn't that precisely what the EPA and other advocates of clean power are engaged in?"

"That's what I thought and what kept me at the EPA for so many years. But when I see how special interests, not economic forces, drive all sorts of unrealistic programs—from bio-fuels like ethanol, which by the way is a carbon disaster, to wind power—I began to lose hope that true transformational progress would emerge."

His comments about ethanol resonated, as our committee had already heard enough testimony about the amount of coal it takes to convert corn to fuel.

"Well, you've given me lots to think about," I say. "Some of what you say makes sense, though. If anything, it seems your arguments bolster Trendle's case for clean, wind-generated power."

He chooses not to respond to that last remark.

"One last question," I ask, as we're about to part. "I ran across a paper recently authored by a Professor Imlen. Ever hear of her?"

Without hesitating, Teddy responds, "She wrote a number of internal papers and memoranda warning the agency about the dangers of nuclear power. She left the department before my time, but people still talk about her pioneering work."

"Did you ever hear what happened to her?"

Rising from his chair, he shrugs. "Like me, she became disillusioned with power politics and cozy relationships between government and big business." Then, a lightbulb clicks on in his head and he adds, "Now that you mention it, I recall that it was something I came across in one of her memoranda that made me begin to see that the carbon conspiracy is real."

I'm stopped in my tracks. I want to know more, but before I can ask, he extends a hand. "Mark, it was great meeting you. And thanks for letting me do a brain dump."

As he turns to walk away, I call out, "Can you stop by Trendle's office next week so we can talk further?"

A smile contradicts his normally serious demeanor. "Gladly, I'll call your office to set up an appointment."

I'm not a devotee of conspiracy theories. There are far simpler explanations for what drives the darker side of humanity—namely greed, pleasure, and lust for power. But Teddy's parting words, combined with the accusation in the Imlen paper and the nonsense about reporting all my phone calls has me wondering if a conspiracy exists in this case. My anxiety level jumps a notch as I ponder who could be behind it.

ELEVEN

The subtleties of the causes and remedies for environmental damage are cast aside on this day. Trendle uses the annual Earth Day lovefest as a golden opportunity to speak to cheering crowds at several of the big, outdoor rallies. As in the past, he makes a rousing speech in the morning at New York's Central Park. Taking advantage of the time zones, he speaks to the zealots who descend upon the Presidio at the base of the Golden Gate Bridge in San Francisco later that afternoon. He spends the subsequent three weeks resting, recharging his political batteries within the warm embrace of his donors, and traveling from one testimonial dinner to the next.

I devote this time to sifting through all the briefings, white papers, brochures, scientific journals, and gifts from green advocates who want to show their love for Trendle.

We are successfully tearing down the god of fossil fuel while proclaiming a better tomorrow by worshipping the gods of renewable energy. With Trendle away, I'm able to enjoy a rare period of quiet on the Hill, especially with Congress out of session and representatives back home, kissing up to the voters. I kick back, relax, and let my thoughts wander.

Shortly before 9:00 p.m. on Monday, just as I'm getting ready to leave, Shauna pokes her head into my office to say good night.

She is one of the unsung heroes that every organization has. She's the first to arrive in the morning and often the last to leave. Shauna performs countless mundane tasks we dump on her, never complaining and always ready to take on more. She hesitates in a fashion that I've come to know. Something's bothering her.

"What's up, Shauna? It looks like you have something on your mind." I chide her a bit. "Don't tell me you've gotten Trendle in trouble."

"Oh no," she replies, wide-eyed. "I would never do anything to harm the congressman's reputation." She's been working for Trendle for fifteen years and still always refers to him as the congressman.

"My fiancé and I have been arguing about the whole carbon-footprint issue."

I am surprised that she mentions her fiancé, Albert. Last year, when Shauna came to work one day wearing a smile that would give Julia Roberts a run for her money and an engagement ring to boot, we were shocked. She's as plain as can be, extremely shy, and works a hundred hours a week.

We had her figured for a lifelong spinster. And try as we might, we've never been able to find out much about him.

The one time he came to the office, Albert—never Al or Bert—wore ripped jeans, a T-shirt with some obscure math symbols on it, canvas sneakers, and his hair hung down over his eyes. He's tall and extremely thin. We figure he's some kind of geeky researcher, but since he spoke even less than Shauna does, we learned very little from him.

"Did you know Albert is a PhD candidate at Georgetown, specializing in meteorological mathematics?" Shauna asks.

That explains the T-shirt. "Shauna, sit down and tell me what's on your mind." She's very nervous and clearly uneasy.

"Mark, you know I'm totally loyal to the congressman and would never do anything to embarrass him."

I try to reassure her, thinking she's responding to my jibe about getting Trendle in trouble. But that isn't it.

Mustering up her courage, she says, "Albert and I talk a lot about what the congressman is doing to raise awareness about the disastrous effects of global warming. For the past year, Albert has been telling me that, from a scientific perspective, the theory of global warming—the effects of the carbon footprint and the danger of greenhouse gases—is pure, political, horse do-do."

I suspect Albert used a different word. I hold up my hand to stop her. "Come on, Shauna, you're beginning to sound like the oil companies." I'm starting to get hot under the collar. "You've seen all the reports and testimony from hundreds of scientists over the years. And you always cheer along with us as we watch Al Gore's *An Inconvenient Truth*." We've probably seen it twenty-five times since it was released. "Not to disrespect Albert, but what qualifies a graduate student to challenge the experts?"

She looks as if she's about to cry. At that, I immediately cool down, pat her hand, and apologize. "You know that Trendle and I trust you completely," I say with sympathy in my voice. "Tell me what Albert says."

"Well, when Albert talks about this stuff, one thing he keeps coming back to is that most scientists here and in Europe refuse to acknowledge the hard evidence of the world's historic weather and temperature patterns over the last two thousand years."

She catches me off guard with that one. I've seen a few of the charts showing the wide swing in mean temperatures at different periods. And, while they've given me moments of uneasiness, I quickly forget them in the electrically charged atmosphere of the global warming debates.

"I would love it if you could meet with Albert for just fifteen minutes. He can explain it better than I."

Her pleading look breaks down my defenses. "OK, Shauna. You own the schedule. Pencil him in for some time this week."

Two days later, I'm in the middle of preparing draft legislation that Trendle wants to move through committee once Congress is back in session. This draft demands a further 40 percent reduction in carbon emissions from automobiles. If a 20 percent reduction passes, we declare victory; if 10 percent passes, then progress has been made. Such is the world I work in.

I'm using Trendle's office, since he's out of town. The receptionist, covering while Shauna is at lunch, pokes her head through the doorway to say my next appointment, Albert Consolvas, is waiting for me. The clueless look on my face prompts her to remind me that Mr. Consolvas is Shauna's fiancé.

"Oh, yeah," I respond without enthusiasm. "Send him in."

A mop of hair on top of a beanpole greets me.

"Albert, nice to see you again,"

We awkwardly shake hands. He sits down on the edge of the couch and I take the chair at the other end of the coffee table. After thirty seconds of strained silence, I realize that for Albert, the halls of Congress, or in this case congressional office buildings, are another planet with alien life-forms scampering about. He sits, legs crossed at the ankles, with both hands under his thighs, looking around at all the office memorabilia through his rimless glasses. Shauna's egghead genius has no idea what to do or say.

Trying to break the ice, I remark, "That symbol on your shirt is interesting. Does it represent your fraternity?" It looked like half a box with the number one and a dash in front of it. As the words left my mouth, it struck me that no normal fraternity would let this guy in the door. And his response confirms that.

"Mr. Burnham—"

"Please call me Mark."

He pauses for a moment, chuckling. "That's funny, Mark." He looks up, sees the blank stare on my face, and realizes that I really don't have a clue. "Sorry. I forget some people aren't into mathematics."

Well, that's an understatement. I avoid math at all cost. In fact, the only numbers of real importance to me are football scores and Trendle's polls.

"This symbol is the square root of negative one. It is the entry point to the incredible world of complex numbers."

At this point, I'm thinking that Shauna and Albert together is complex enough.

"Numbers aren't my specialty. Anyway, what can I do for you? Shauna tells me you have some information related to global warming."

With that puzzled look he's worn since he arrived, Albert blurts out, "Isn't someone supposed to swear me in or something?"

I smile as it dawns on me that he thinks this is some sort of hearing.

"We reserve that for formal hearings. In fact, informal discussions such as this help us gather important background information. You may speak freely. This is strictly off the record."

The tension visibly drains from his face. "Well, you see, Mr.…er uh Mark, I've reviewed the ambient air and water temperatures recorded by Columbus, Vespucci, Cabot, Hudson, Scott, Darwin, and a host of other explorers from their voyages of discovery. The mean, median, and standard deviation prove that there have been huge swings in temperature compared to the eighth century. At that time, Greenland really was green. Nordic farmers raised hay and grazed cattle on the island. Following that period, the Earth went into a Mini Ice Age and it actually stayed pretty cold until about a century ago, when mean temperatures started to rise."

He goes on. After five minutes, my head is swimming as it becomes apparent that Albert lacks the ability to summarize, headline, or frame an issue for the uninitiated. "Slow down. Let me see if I understand. You're saying that over the last 1,500 years, there have been wide swings in temperature that have nothing to do with increased carbon levels in the atmosphere?"

Albert looks at me as if I have the plague. "Yeah. That's what I just said."

I'm tempted to let this pass, but the challenge is too great. "Why couldn't the changes have been caused by corresponding variations in carbon levels? Who would know?"

Albert's jumping up and down in his seat, hair every which way, as he emphatically shakes his head. "No, no, no, the proof's in the glaciers! It's all about depth and longitudinal positioning within the ice and snow."

At this point, I'm thoroughly lost. It also occurs to me that my education regarding climate change is lopsided. I know all there is to know, at least politically, about carbon and methane levels, the multiple ways fossil fuels pollute, and the fact that sooner or later we will burn them all up.

I also know that without a strategic renewable-energy policy, America's future is in jeopardy. On the other hand, I know little about historical trends and I care less, as it does not grab the attention of the American public.

"OK, Albert, assume you're trying to explain this to a fourth-grade C student," which is how I feel now.

He takes a deep breath and closes his eyes. After a moment, I'm ready to reach over and wake him, thinking he has fallen asleep.

"My apologies," he says, as he sits back on the couch. "I'm so used to just picking up the discussion with professors that I'm forgetting to provide background."

In that admission I catch a hint of why Shauna is attracted to him. Like her, he seems to have no hidden agenda. What you see is what you get.

"OK, let's try this," he says. "When you were a kid, you had lots of toys."

I nod. My parents were always giving me educational toys, games, and train sets at Christmas and on my birthday.

"But you didn't get them all at once," he continues. "I'll bet every time you got a new toy or game, the old ones went into the toy chest or closet and were quickly forgotten as the new ones were thrown on top of them."

Since Mary Poppins didn't live at my house, he's right.

"If you decide one day to clean out all the toys, beginning with the newest ones, you would have a kind of history of your toy experiences. You would see what you liked to play with at different ages, what toys were popular at different times, and so forth."

"So you're telling me that a glacier is like the toy chest," I respond. "Not sure I see the connection, since glaciers are essentially one big ice cube."

He's really animated now and smiles. "That's what most people think. But glaciers are filled with human artifacts: stone and metal tools, arrows, animal-skin clothing, not to mention trees and vegetation trapped in the ice. Glaciers also hold the remains of birds, insects, and mammals, including humans."

I mention the news a few years back of someone finding a hunter believed to be 10,000 years old in the Swiss Alps. Researchers dubbed him Otzi, the Ice Man.

"That's right. And these remains are rich in environmental evidence."

He goes on for another ten minutes, describing the carbon markers, evidence of pollution going back thousands of years, the size of tree rings, pollutants in frozen animal remains, dental characteristics of mammal teeth, structure and chemical makeup of bird feathers, and so on.

"Albert, I think I get it. You could theoretically develop a kind of environmental history. But how do you date the items?"

"That's the best part," he exclaims. "Glaciers are essentially extremely slow-moving, frozen rivers. Depending on how deep within the glacier and how high up in the flow an item is, one can date it within fifty years.

"So the focus of your PhD is building such a history?" I ask.

He starts to laugh in his geeky way, confirming my lack of knowledge in this area.

"Oh, no. There've been countless studies and sound scientific research conducted in this area over the past seventy-five years. The abundant evidence from all of this, combined with various historical records uncovered over the last two thousand years, makes it clear that there have been wide swings in median temperatures, rainfall, and weather patterns in general, and they've spanned decades—even centuries. The Medieval Warm Period lasted from 800 to 1300 AD. It was during this period that the Vikings colonized Greenland, as the seas were ice-free. These colonies died out during the Mini Ice Age that occurred in stages between the sixteenth and mid-nineteenth centuries."

Albert is on a roll. "Next time you're on Hilton Head Island playing golf, go to the Coastal Discover Museum. On the wall is a map that illustrates how, 50,000 years ago, the island was almost completely underwater as the seas were fifteen feet higher at the time and have since then gradually gone down."

"Wait," I interrupt, feeling defensive. "I've been in the middle of every major environmental debate going back to my college days and it's generally accepted that historical evidence should be discounted since the world today is vastly different due to the impact of fossil fuels."

With another chuckle, Albert says, "Oh, the Gore Groupies," his moniker for anyone who has gotten religious over the evils of fossil fuels and carbon pollution, "have shunned the obvious but apparently not politically engaging wealth of evidence. In short, they choose to downplay it."

I'm still skeptical but decide not to push further, as my next appointment, some dull but important lobbyist fund-raiser, is waiting. "I have another meeting, but I'm curious, what exactly is your doctoral thesis focused on?"

"My goal is to apply the discipline of mathematics to sort out and catalog the numerous and subtle correlation coefficients among the thousands of factors that affect climate." We shake hands and I promise to consider the information he's shared. The nagging sense that I've missed something all these years moves in and out of my conscience throughout the rest of the day.

Albert and Teddy have something in common. They both chose to challenge simplistic answers to complex problems. They have done so by tackling dull, uninspiring evidence in the hope that someone will listen. Clearly, both of them have valid points to make. And I'm prepared to listen further, especially to Teddy. However, it still seems clear to me that while many factors are in play, the fundamental truth remains the same: carbon pollution is the chief cause of global warming.

TWELVE

I've been home for two hours and I am still shaking like a leaf, even after three beers.

I left the office deep in thought, Albert's remarks fresh on my mind. I called Chet from one of the few pay phones left in the Capitol complex. He still hasn't been able to discover who is behind my tailing, which is now routine. Just as I was stepping off the curb on Independence, I heard the blare of a car horn. Looking up, I saw a taxi bearing down on me at high speed, and I froze. At the last moment, a hand grabbed me by the collar and pulled me to safety.

"Hey buddy, you're lucky that guy didn't kill you. These taxi drivers are maniacs."

In shock from the near hit, I nod dumbly as he continued, "You should be more careful when stepping into the unknown."

As he walked away, it struck me that his last remark was an odd one. I looked around and noticed that the person tailing me was not the least bit concerned as he sat on a bench pretending to read the paper.

Then it hit me like a sledgehammer. This was no accident, but a well-planned warning that I was treading on somebody's toes. But whose?

As I sit on the couch pondering the situation, my cell rings. It's Bernie, Professor Longworth's grad student.

"Mark, I talked with the professor, and he thought it was a good idea if the two of us exchanged information."

Not wanting him to say too much in case someone was listening, I cut in.

"Hey, Bernie. Great to hear from you. Listen, this fantasy hockey thing is out of control. Now our buddy is suddenly elevated to professor just because he beat us last season. Let's grab a beer at Monroe's and figure out our strategy."

Before he can answer, I hang up, grab my keys, and run out the door. Monroe's is a sports bar across from Union Station. Since Bernie is a student, he undoubtedly knows the place. Sure enough, ten minutes after I get there, he sits at the bar next to me.

"Just listen. I had to cut you off because it's likely someone is tapping my phones."

The look of confusion on his face turns to fear. "What the hell are you talking about?"

I decide I need to trust this guy and brief him on what's been going on for the last few weeks.

"I don't know if I want to get involved," he says after taking it all in. The agitation is apparent in his body language.

"Calm down and try to look like you're having a good time." I order a couple of beers and continue. "It's too late. You and the professor are involved whether you like it or not. Remember, it was you guys who dumped that headline on my desk."

Reluctantly, he asks, "What do you want us to do?"

"Connie Imlen was an academic working on renewable energy issues when she conveniently died shortly after sending me a very disturbing report in which she accused a certain company of highly unethical and most certainly illegal tactics to undermine the environmentalists."

"What was she implicating the company for?"

"The sin as old as time itself: greed."

I gave him the particulars regarding Con-Gen and he promised to see what Longworth and he could find out.

THIRTEEN

Events over the next several weeks keep me happily distracted and on the road almost continuously. Three fund-raisers dominate the time. The first is sponsored by Friends of Trendle. Whenever I get around this crew, I can't help thinking that with friends like these, who cares about enemies. They are the local chamber of commerce and vineyard growers association. Wine lends a healthy glow to such events and loosens the tongue as well as the pocketbook.

In short order, Trendle learns that taxes on wine are too high, restrictions on interstate wine sales are obsolete, and synthetic corks are the wave of the future. The anti-cork guy spends every moment championing the environmental benefits of saving cork trees, never mind that synthetic cork is yet another derivative of petroleum.

The real friends, of course, are the ever-faithful WW9, who are looking for new and inventive ways to circumvent the limits on campaign financing. Monsieur Cork had little interest in Trendle or his politics until Liddy managed to charm the second-biggest vintner in the region into switching to synthetic corks. Suddenly, the cork guy and thirty of his closest friends decide to take an interest in Trendle's political future by forking over several thousand apiece to top off the campaign war chest.

As I do at all these events, I hang off to the side and continue the dialogue with attendees after the congressman listens carefully to their concerns while stroking their egos. It's my job to triage these folks in such a manner as to limit Trendle's exposure to only the most important of them. Sometimes they are not too sharp. The cork guy is as dumb as the product he sells. He proceeds to confide in me how happy he is that Liddy and the Rumple Sisters are investing heavily in his company's stock. Not only is it better for me not to know this illegal piece of information, it also means that on subsequent visits to this West Coast paradise, they will be twisting my arm gently to support expansive use of synthetic corks via tax credits.

The second event is very a private dinner at an exclusive restaurant, The Tablet. Con-Gen's PAC wants to share its love for Trendle. General Clarkson hosts this one. Intimate events such as these are very informal and completely off the record. It's all about strengthening the bonds of political friendship. And contrary to the opinion of cynics, a surprising number of these friendships are real. Clarkson has developed a deep bond with Al Clampton, VP of Government Relations at Con-Gen. Their relationship reaches back to their time at West Point. Al is the only person I've ever seen T.C. loosen up with. At this event, I found them back on the patio smoking cigars and laughing about some old incident from their procurement days.

As the evening ends, I stand just outside the door as Trendle thanks each attendee with a warm handshake and a winning smile. Most of them barely acknowledge my presence as I say good-bye. Al Clampton must have had a few too many, as he's looser than normal. When I offer my hand, he grabs it and pumps furiously while grinning like a kid who knows he ate too much ice cream. "Hey, boy," he slurs, "you should thank your stars you're on Trendle's team."

I smile and nod as he goes on. "You gotta love this carbon-conspiracy stuff."

I freeze at the remark as he stumbles out the door. It reminds me of Connie Imlen's paper and Teddy Edelstein's parting words about a carbon conspiracy. When I get back to DC, I'll need to reengage with Teddy pronto.

The event I always look forward to is the annual Artists for Trendle gala at the Preston Wind Research Institute. As usual, Malcolm Little's charity supporting struggling artists is the sponsor this year. Due to the special status of the research center, many of the normal rules of fundraising don't apply. The center itself funds the dinner, as it is a combination fund-raiser and show featuring emerging artists from around the country. It's no coincidence that a very high number of these artists are spouses or children of

Hollywood celebrities and corporate executives. With rare exceptions, their work has one thing in common: it's awful.

Trendle is busy with Malcolm and a starlet who managed to take up modern art between DUI convictions. I've concluded that modern art was invented so that anyone with too much time and money on his hands could call himself an artist. Of course, the real story is that anyone with money to burn and the desire to call himself "creative" will discover that if he and his corporate PAC donate to Trendle, he happens to receive an invitation to show his work.

The banquet room is packed with works on display and hundreds of wannabe artists, all drooling over each others' creations and stroking each others' egos with memorable phrases such as, "You captured the essence of the angst mankind experiences consuming meat." Never mind that filet and lobster are the main course. Why argue with artistic logic?

I'm milling around enjoying the circus and laughing to myself at how gullible these suckers are. Dinner includes the usual speeches and awards presented to promising new artists of the year. Trendle expresses his rousing support for this artistic community so devoted to the environment and his campaign account.

As the event is winding down and Malcolm and Trendle are bidding their guests good night, Liddy slips up behind me, takes my hand in hers, and whispers, "Come along, Mark. I have someone who wants to meet you."

As we walk through the outdoor garden, I chide her a bit. "Now don't you try and take advantage of me, Liddy."

She looks over her shoulder, flashes that million-dollar smile, and purrs, "Oh don't I wish, but I know better with you. I want you to meet someone I know you'll find interesting."

As we approach, a woman turns to face us and holds out her hand. "Hello, Mr. Burnham. It's very nice to meet you."

She's drop-dead gorgeous. I find my attention immediately focused on her as Liddy walks away. I barely hear her say, "I'll leave you two alone to get to know one another better."

"My name is Chloe Sullivan and my boss told me to make sure I met you."

Without realizing it, I'm so intently focused on her that she's becoming uncomfortable.

"Mr. Burnham, is there something wrong?"

The directness of her question shakes me out of my reverie. "No, of course not. Call me Mark," I quickly continue. "And who did you say your boss was?"

"As a matter of fact I didn't, but since you ask, I report personally to Mr. Davidson." Lucas K. Davidson is managing partner of Becht, Chalmers & Davidson, a highly successful law firm and important supporter of Trendle's. I know him well, as I often hear from Lucas, who invariably says something like this: "Mark, you know how damaging false and misleading stories are about the wealthy political supporters. See what you can do to get Trendle to redirect the press's attention elsewhere."

I pass the word on to Trendle. He calls a press conference and drops some red herring of an accusation that redirects the media away from the Prestons—the family name of the Rumple Sisters. While the sisters seem harmless, their wealth is built on old money and they are zealous in working to avoid public scandal. One time, when it looked like the Prestons were going to be indicted for securities fraud, Trendle announced in a press conference that he had just received information that Anthony Rosetto, California's attorney general, was under investigation for insider trading. It didn't matter that it was untrue. It served the purpose of tainting the AG's reputation sufficiently that the media lost interest in the Preston indictment, which shortly thereafter was dropped. Trendle's office then issued an apology, saying that the information on Rosetto turned out to be untrue. But by then, of course, it was too late.

Given Lucas's reputation as a womanizer, it occurs to me that someone as young and attractive as Chloe might be providing highly personalized assistance of the non-legal kind to him. But as she talked about her background, experience, and duties at the firm, it's apparent that her job is real and of considerable importance.

She's responsible for analyzing the political impact of possible lawsuits the firm considers pursuing. This is no small matter. In the wake of recent criminal retaliation and jail time for senior partners of firms engaged in inventing class-action suits based on fraudulent medical evidence, the firm has become especially cautious. After all, it's no use earning millions of dollars in legal fees if you're not free to enjoy it. They're not above pushing the limits by promoting questionable lawsuits so long as the evidence is real.

The courts themselves are ruled by judges, almost all of whom are former attorneys striving to salt away a healthy nest egg. Thus, the courts tend to bend over backward to support all manner of lawsuits—from the profound to the absurd. It's when law firms venture into the outright manufacturing of evidence that the voting public finally catches on and rebels, even in tort-friendly states, such as Louisiana.

While Chloe's title is senior research analyst, as we talk I discover she's an attorney licensed to practice in California, New York, and DC. She has a law degree from Yale, served as editor of the law review, and for two years clerked for Associate Supreme Court Justice Edward Kensington. Given Kensington's young age, he's expected to serve many years on the court. Because he's a centrist who is driven by pragmatism rather than ideology, he has cast the deciding vote on a host of issues. Of particular interest to him is the appeal of monetary awards from class-action lawsuits.

Indeed, the charming Ms. Sullivan has friends in high places. Chloe is beautiful, fit, and self-assured without being overbearing. That by itself is no big deal, as half of the junior staffers on the Hill meet that description. What makes her so attractive comes from something deeper. As she shares her background and current work and comments about the partners she works for, it hits me. We have a lot in common. She's as passionate as I am concerning our respective interests. It is refreshing to talk politics with someone who is not trying to garner a favor. Spending the bulk of my time with politicians, most of whom are also lawyers, I seldom get a straight answer. There is always the unspoken agenda and whispered invitation: I'll scratch your back if you scratch mine.

As we continue to talk, I became increasingly engaged beyond simply having a professional interest. We laugh about the quirks of the partners at Becht, and I, of course, have a wealth of stories going back to my intern days with Senator Slade. She smiles when I mention the senator's breakfast-in-bed program for mentoring the youngest, cutest, and most clueless interns who paraded through his office. And I'm not surprised when she admits to receiving several similar invitations over the years. I ask her how she handles them.

"I've come to accept that some otherwise well-balanced alpha males who are successful in their careers have huge egos that need attention," she calmly shares. "It never bothers me the first time a guy hits on me. I simply blow him off with a laugh."

"And if he tries again?"

"The second time I tell him he's too old for me. That deflates the egos of most of them." She gives me a flinty look and goes on to explain, "Since they're all married, if one of them tries a third time I simply say, 'If you want to take me to dinner, fine. But as soon as you leave, I'll be sure to call your wife and invite her too, as I'm sure you wouldn't want any rumors of scandal to tarnish the firm's reputation.'"

I nearly choke on my drink at that. "I bet that works," I say when I finally stop laughing.

"Always," she says with a wink. "All the regular wolves hit on me when I first joined the firm. After they finally struck out, they started to drop by my office to pour out their woes regarding money, wives, ex-wives, girlfriends, alimony, and anything else that was perpetually threatening their existence. It seems I've become something of a combination mother and sister to them."

"Thank God you're an attorney, since some of the info you pick up could be used to blackmail them."

During the course of our conversation, Chloe wants to know what I do for Trendle. I take her on a meandering journey beginning with college, where my militant love affair with the environment began. I fill her in on my internship with Slade and the last several years with Trendle. I ramble a lot longer than I normally would, as I don't want her to leave. After what seems like only a matter of minutes, all the guests are gone and the evening too quickly ends.

"Mark, it was very nice talking with you," she says, as she shakes my hand. "Perhaps next time I'm in DC I'll give you a call and we can have dinner."

"I would like that very much!"

As she walks away, I figure Chloe is just being polite but hope that she isn't.

Another successful event recharging the WW9 and Trendle's extensive network of supporters is successfully executed. It's time to head back to DC.

Usually, I stay behind a day or two to conduct district business. But this time, I ride back with the congressman. As we sit in the luxuriously appointed Lear jet owned by Malcolm Little, I can't help but marvel that with all the oversight, Congressman Trendle is still able to use the jet at no cost—not to mention the carbon pollution pouring out of the two jet engines. Of course, officially, it's owned by the nonprofit that helps struggling artists by ferrying them and their works to various exclusive art exhibits around the country. Little always makes sure we have one of them along. The artist and whatever grotesque piece of work he or she is showing are relegated to the after cabin, while we enjoy the finer amenities up front. It's not only a testament to Trendle's influence in Congress, but also to the reality that he undoubtedly would continue to be reelected by his district even if he was found guilty of murder. (In fact, he would probably gain votes if the victim were a polluter.)

As we glide across the continent at 39,000 feet, drinks in hand, Trendle begins retelling old political war stories in which he's invariably the hero. I'm only half listening when he suddenly grows quiet, his normally cast-iron confidence gone. Perhaps it's the third drink he's nursing, but what comes out of his mouth stuns me.

"You know, Mark, sometimes I can't help wondering if climate change is real."

I'm at a loss for words. The moment quickly passes and he's back to his normal, boisterous self. I'm in shock. I am passionate about my deeply held beliefs, so this hint of doubt from someone I consider a mentor and an icon in the battle against the catastrophic consequences of global warming is traumatizing. Questions rage in my head. Why did he say that? What has happened that prompted this? Is this new or is Trendle expressing long-standing doubt?

I'd intended to use the flight to grill him about what he knows concerning who's following me, Melanie's sudden departure, and Connie's death. My intent was to pin him down and discover the truth. But his remark has taken the wind out of my sails. I'm wondering if he is behind all of this. Then it hits me. Did Trendle say that to see how I would react? The anxiety has returned big time.

The rest of the flight is a bummer. I've always been a person of action wanting to know what is behind every question. My research instincts are kicking in. I'm eager to get back to DC and start working the phones, surfing the web, and tracking back through Trendle's public statements to see if I can find a hint as to what's behind his remark. And I definitely need to connect with Southers to kick this investigation into high gear.

I've long been convinced that global warming is a real and looming danger. How could it not be? Mainstream scientists around the world agree. Even the major oil companies have signed on, figuring they can still make billions from oil while paying lip service to a greener future. Since all evidence points to the obvious truth of our cause, what I really want to find out is the source of Trendle's doubt. It's not the words themselves that are driving my need to know, it's the hint of guilt I heard in his voice that really concerns me. Further, this reawakens the turmoil brought on by the insight Teddy and Albert shared.

As we make our final approach into National, the same thought keeps repeating itself in my head. The science of global warming is settled. The evidence is in. What can Trendle possibly feel guilty about?

FOURTEEN

Spring semester of senior year, I landed an internship with the state's junior senator, Calvin Slade. I accepted the position after carefully reviewing the political blogs, which assured me he was next in line for sainthood. How wrong I was. Senator Slade was in his mid fifties and boasted a thick head of silver and black hair, immaculately groomed, that screamed: this guy knows what he is talking about. It sat on top of a ruggedly handsome face that perpetually wore a boyish grin. His trim, athletic frame draped with three thousand-dollar suits and Gucci slip-ons radiated the kind of power that's irresistible to many women. It helped explain why he consistently won reelection with 70-plus percent of the female voters solidly behind him.

Cal, as he insisted we call him, simultaneously embodied the highest principles of service in the public forum and the lowest when it came to private affairs. He generally began his day having breakfast in bed with the newest, star-struck intern in his office. Yet by the end of the semester, even as a committed Democrat, I'd gained a grudging respect for Cal's no-nonsense, centrist Republican stance. He never confused principles with ego. While he was willing to support the one, when practical, he quickly abandoned the other to achieve consensus and obtain the necessary votes.

As much as I came to admire Senator Slade, he wasn't the politician for me. As I moved between the two chambers of Congress, conveying draft language and messages among the leadership, I came to appreciate the grittiness of the House of Representatives. It really is the people's chamber. Since members of the House run for office every two years, legislating and campaigning are joined at the hip. Members never take their eyes off local issues and the needs of the citizens in their districts. Those who did so would risk losing their seats to unknowns who would latch onto a neglected issue and ride it to victory.

The fact of the matter is that the energy of the House is intoxicating. The men and women who hold these positions of power are as diverse a collection of personalities and perspectives as you will find anywhere. They range from the articulate to the fumbling; the filthy rich to those barely able to cover the DC rent; the idealist to the sleaziest operator. Invariably, though, they share two things. The first is the desire to bring home the pork to their district in whatever fashion speaks to voters: tax reduction in the populated states, jobs in the rust belt, grants to fight urban blight in the large cities, or farm subsidies for the agro communities. The second is frustration with the Senate's Mount Olympus air of superiority and its uncanny ability to bring even the most promising legislation to a grinding halt. Of course, at any given moment, a third of the members are trying to move to the other wing of the Capitol.

I spent much of my last semester carefully researching House members, looking for someone thoroughly dedicated to fighting for the environment. In addition, he or she needed the political juice to make things happen. As luck would have it, Congressman Trendle, who was already on my short list, read my senior thesis on the damaging effects of carbon. My professor had insisted that each senior submit his or her paper to an authority on the subject with the hopes that person would read it and respond. The fact that Trendle not only reviewed it but also added comments and questions was an enormous ego booster. He wanted me on his staff and knew what button to push to assure that I would jump at the chance. Even though I later learned the handwritten comments actually were written by Shauna, I was hooked.

My first day on the job, I nervously stood as Trendle walked into the office. "Take a seat."

I squeezed into the only available chair between Jeremy Schienman, a lawyer; and T.C. Clarkson.

"It's Mark, right?" asked Trendle. Without waiting for an answer, he four-barreled me. "Listen, you're a smart kid. Tell me what your top priority is."

"To carry out research projects that you or your senior staff assigns."

"Wrong! Kid, your job is to protect my ass. You only have a job so long as I remain in office."

Seeing the confused look on my face, he turned to Jeremy. "Brief him on the crisis unfolding." With that, Trendle stormed out of the office.

Conveying the demeanor of a fashion designer and the lofty air confined to aficionados of fine wine, Jeremy said, "Mark, the congressman is under attack. His enemies are charging him with serious ethics violations. Unless you make them go away, he and, by association, you are out of a job and your career is finished."

The voice inside my head screamed, "Why is this my problem? Run out of here as fast as you can." But Schienman's intensity and General Clarkson's cane, which was raised in a threatening manner, had me glued to the seat.

"If you fix this problem, your career will take off."

Clarkson jumped in. "The House ethics committee has charged Trendle with two counts of misuse of campaign funds and accepting bribes from influential donors." Clarkson's eyes bored into mine like two lasers. "The charges are complete fabrications. We know it and the committee knows it. Your job is to dig up the evidence that proves his innocence."

Jeremy took the lead and for the next ninety minutes, briefed me on the specifics.

"Jeremy, I need to interview every one of his supporters and collect any documentation there is supporting Trendle's innocence," I said with more self-assurance than I felt.

"You're already booked on a flight to the West Coast. The WW9 have been alerted. You'll meet them at the club." Noticing my confusion, Jeremy elaborated. "Wise & Wealthy Nine is Trendle's affectionate moniker for the core group of nine powerful supporters to whom he pays special attention. The ethics charges mention several of them by name."

With that, he handed me a packet of info. As they left the office, Clarkson turned and with pointed cane said, "Son, remember what I said."

"That I'm the sacrificial lamb if this goes south."

"Trendle's right. You're a smart boy."

I looked up to see Shauna standing in the doorway, tickets in hand. "You'd better head to the airport." The expression on her face was not encouraging.

Cruising across the continent, alone with my thoughts, I concluded that my only chance was to proceed as if success was assured and hope for the best. The documents Clarkson handed me included biographies along with photos of the WW9.

Lydia Van Flugete, or Liddy as she prefers, was the first one I met. She is the queen of the WW9 and her picture didn't do her justice. She's far more beautiful in person.

"So you're Tom's boy. It's fabulous that you're able to brief us at our monthly caucus." I quickly discovered Liddy loved using political terms to describe her tea parties for the rich. "You can enlighten us regarding the nasty accusations being hurled at our beloved congressman!" Normally, these monthly events take place poolside at her ranch (really an equestrian retreat overlooking the Pacific). However, given the serious nature of the charges, she'd elected to use the club room at The Wind Research Institute.

"I'm Mark Burnham. Congressman Trendle asked me to speak with you regarding the ethics charges he is facing." I briefed them on the specifics. While I spoke, I noticed three elderly women whispering back and forth with a man.

At the mention of damage to their reputations, a man spoke up. "Mark, are you saying we could be in trouble simply because we generously support Trendle?" He turned out to be Malcolm Little, the only one of the nine whose bio did not include a picture.

"Unfortunately Mr. Little—"

"Call me Malcolm."

"Malcolm, it's a distinct possibility. The insider trading charges suggest that Trendle was handing over information to someone who benefited from it in the stock market."

"And who might that someone be?"

A hush fell over the room as they waited for a reply. "Individuals were not identified. However, a syndicate of Central American banks figured prominently in the investigation."

"So why is Trendle worried?"

I hesitated for a moment.

"Mark," Liddy remarked. "I'm sure that regardless of who it is, we have the talent and resources to take care of it."

"Con-Gen Industries was mentioned as an intermediary that facilitated the movement of money from the banks into the exchanges through its corporate brokerage accounts. Not surprisingly, the noise is coming from the Republican leadership."

A smile slowly appeared on Malcolm's face. "Mark, I'm confident that the charges are baseless and I'm sure they will disappear of their own accord."

Malcolm Little is a self-proclaimed artist in his late thirties. His works periodically surface at exclusive galleries around the country. He's a trim figure, with dark wavy hair, piercing eyes, and carefully manicured hands. Malcolm, who dresses as if he were ready to tee off at some charity golf event, always seems to be hiding something. He's articulate, smooth, and publicity shy, preferring the intimacy of the small gathering, the whispered one-on-one conversation, and the phone conferences that demand his attention day and night. Malcolm is also a collector of some note, gathering pieces from around the world. His taste is varied and always interesting. Since joining WW9, he has lent many pieces of art for display at the Wind Research Institute. The big mystery is the source of the seemingly endless wealth supporting his extravagant lifestyle, which includes homes in France and Italy and a penthouse suite in Hong Kong, as well as the continuous additions of art to his collection. Malcolm's presence at Liddy's monthly gatherings is significant. He doesn't waste words on the trivial, unless it is to brag about his newest artistic creation. Otherwise, his conversation generally focuses on some piece of legislation, unrelated to the environment, that he expects Trendle to support.

In addition to his other duties, Trent Watersworth, Trendle's district manager, spends significant amounts of time engineering legislative favors for Malcolm. He sits on the board of numerous NGOs that, according to rumor, are largely funded by him. They publish a variety of position papers and political endorsements. The name Malcolm Little never appears on any of them.

"Mark, I believe we understand the seriousness of the charges. Reassure the congressman that we have the situation under control," Malcolm said.

He turned to Davidson. "Lucas, it seems we should be able to clarify any irregularities, don't you think?"

Lucas K. Davidson, managing partner of do-we-cheatem-and-steal, or as they are officially known, Becht, Chalmers & Davidson, is all olive oil and ever on his game. His firm leads the country in launching innovative class-action suits against polluters. For a time, the firm even explored filing suit against the tobacco companies due to the impact of second-hand smoke on the quality of life of canines and felines (aka household pets). It ran up against a brick wall when someone pointed out that the pets would of necessity also be suing their owners, and since the owners would have to initiate the suit on behalf of these domestic plaintiffs, the idea was quickly dropped. Lucas is ruggedly handsome in his mid-fifties and embraces everyone he meets with hale and hearty good cheer. But as I've learned, one needs to be careful. While Lucas is stroking your ego, he is picking your pocket in search of the next class-action lawsuit.

"I'll have the firm prepare a report detailing the care taken to ensure that any and all trading activities even remotely connected to this group are free from improper influence."

The remaining members of WW9 are undistinguished except for their wealth. As long as Liddy is backing Trendle, their support is assured. They all hope that by association, political fairy dust will fall upon them, thus invigorating their otherwise dull lives. Since fund-raising is the vital lubricant of a political career, Trendle is more than happy to sprinkle whatever magic they want to believe in.

Malcolm is the one WW9 member who worries Trendle. He has had several conversations with Liddy about wanting to avoid any political scandal in connection with Malcolm's mysterious wealth and the favors he is always asking of Trendle. Politicians hate the unknown, especially if it could taint their careers. In fact, one of my first tasks when I signed on to team Trendle was conducting research into the source of Malcolm's wealth. After two weeks of surfing public records on the Internet and working the phones with trusted friends of Trendle's, I had little (no pun intended) to show other than obscure international corporate ties and significant minority stock holdings in a number of Fortune 500 companies. At that point, Trendle abruptly ordered me to drop the research. When I questioned him about the decision, he mumbled, "Let's not annoy one of our most important donors." I suspect one of the "trusted friends" told Malcolm what I was up to.

The showcase backdrop proclaiming WW9's commitment is the Wind Research Institute. Built by Con-Gen, it screams love for the environment. This state-of-the-art center sits on 150 acres of superbly manicured lawn and lush gardens, and includes a beneficiaries-only club. The Institute is, not surprisingly, situated in the heart of Trendle's district. Here, the congressman often holds press conferences while behind him, images of redeemed Nicaraguan rain forests, snowcapped mountains, and of course, tastefully designed windmills, flit across a high-def, eighteen-by-thirty-six-foot screen. Trendle situated his district office in spacious accommodations at the back of the main building. It's a clever choice, ensuring that the scores of constituents seeking favors from him as well as the press experience the promise of the bright future the Institute offers.

As I left the room, Malcolm handed me a manila envelope. "Please be sure to deliver this personally to Trendle."

Sure enough, by week's end, the crisis had passed. The committee suspended the investigation indefinitely.

I looked up from my desk and saw Trendle staring down at me. "Mark, you did an outstanding job taking care of the ethics committee nuisance." I suspected the sealed envelope I'd handed to Trendle on my return is what did it.

"Congressman," I protested. "I'm not sure what I did, exactly."

"You followed orders."

Thus, once a month, like clockwork, I fly into the setting Pacific sun to share the latest Washington wisdom with the Wise & Wealthy Nine. They love the gossip and the snippets of news and scientific breakthroughs, no matter how impractical, I share with them. It all feeds their pipe dream of transforming the world (or at least their little corner of it) into a new Garden of Eden. There are moments when I wonder how this collection of super-rich flakes is able to maintain its purity of commitment to the cause. But it seems that an abundance of resources, financial as opposed to natural, make it possible for them to maintain environmental virginity.

FIFTEEN

A week goes by before I can dig into Trendle's admission of doubt about climate change. The accelerated pace of this year's budget process has every committee working overtime, trying to make sure members have a chance to plug in their favorite pet projects. I'm feeling guilty about going behind Trendle's back. He has been a consistent supporter of mine, advancing me to chief of staff, and I really do look up to him as a mentor. But I have to know. For reasons of self-preservation as well as genuine concern for Trendle, I need to get to the bottom of this.

Normally when I'm searching for a solution to a problem I've been wrestling with, I'll bounce it off one of several staffers I've come to rely on over the years. They understand how Congress works and, more importantly, I trust them to provide sound advice. However, this is no ordinary problem and as much as I value my colleagues' advice, I can't risk having them inadvertently share what I might tell them with others. Finally, I settle on the one person I believe will keep what I share with her in confidence. She was an important mentor when I served as a college-sponsored intern in Congress.

Mabis Flugenstahler, former staff director to Senator Cal Slade, finally retired from the Senate and is now a senior research analyst for the Farragut North Group, a centrist think tank tapped by moneyed interests from both sides of the aisle. It was Mabis who set me straight when I nearly blew the internship with Slade.

It was a something of a shock for me, an idealistic college student, to learn that senators are illiterate. OK, they technically can read, but they avoid it. Two days on the job and this lesson was driven home like a knife in the gut. After studying some innocuous piece of legislation, I fully expected a spirited debate, with Cal and the senior staff thoughtfully weighing the merits of the bill. Mabis, the quintessential Hill staffer, Slade's calendar etched in her brain and ever ready to defend him against all threats foreign and domestic, sat in one chair. Cal took the other and I sat on the couch. He chatted with Mabis for a few minutes about a pending vote, and then abruptly turned to me and said: "Mark…it's Mark, right?" I dumbly nodded. "You know what I'm about. How should I vote?"

In that brief instant of tongue tied-terror, it hit me right between the eyes. Other than his devotion to cute interns and fund-raising, neither of which seemed relevant at the moment, I had no idea what he stood for on this or most other issues. I started to mumble something about Republican principles when Cal silenced me with a raised hand followed by a knowing look at Mabis. She responded, "I will get you a vote recommendation this afternoon."

From then on, I was always prepared.

Mabis was one of the shrewdest staffers on the Hill. She looked just as you imagine a Flugenstahler would: She draped her six-foot-two, Eleanor Roosevelt frame in borderline spinster (which she is not) clothing. Horn-rimmed glasses and tightly pulled-up hair completed the picture. She drilled me on the facts of senatorial life.

"Look, Mark, you're new in this office and the senator will let you slide just this once. But from now on, when I assign you a piece of legislation you must know it thoroughly, know the senator's position on the issue, and be ready to tell him—not suggest—how to vote." She said all this while looking directly at me through her quarter-inch thick glasses.

Given her years in Congress and current position at the think tank, I figure she'll know if there's anything to be concerned about, or at least be able to point me in the right direction. In addition, Mabis cultivates a broad network of influential staff directors, senators, powerful lobbyists, and some ex members of Congress that she can tap into for information. I needed to broach the subject carefully, not only to protect Trendle's reputation, but also to cover my own ass should this get back to him. Knowing she's an early riser, I call her office just after seven. Sure enough, she answers. "Hello, how may I help you?"

"Hey, Mabis, this is Mark Burnham, a blast from the past."

"Mark, how are you?" she says, her voice brightening considerably. "I hear nothing but great stuff about all the political waves you're making on Trendle's behalf. You must be doing something right because Big Oil has you on their list of someone never to invite to the annual Oil Man's gala down in Houston. How long has it been since we've talked?"

"At least four years, other than the occasional wave at fund-raising events."

We engage in the inevitable mandatory gossip about the latest political scandal for a few minutes. Finally, Mabis interrupts. "Mark, you didn't call me at this hour just to gossip. What can I do for you?"

"No," I admit, "I need some specific info and figured if anyone might know, you would."

This is where it becomes tricky. I'm not prepared to share my doubts concerning Trendle's commitment to the environment. It could be nothing more than a fixation on my part. After all, this is the first time in seven years I've heard him waiver on his commitment to a carbon-free world. But I'm under personal attack and it scares me more than it angers me. I don't believe in coincidences. Trendle's doubts, reaction to the Imlen paper, her suspicious death, a sudden interest in whom I speak with on the phone, and being followed tells me it's somehow all connected. Paranoia threatens to consume me. I have to act before it tears me apart.

"Mabis, I'm doing some preventative damage control. We received an anonymous phone call, supposedly from a concerned citizen in Trendle's district, accusing him of being a fraud, suggesting I look into his early years."

"So what? We received lots of crank calls while I was on the Hill and simply thanked the caller and ignored him."

This is where I get creative. "Normally, I'd do the same. But the caller seemed to know a lot about Trendle's history and alluded to cozy relationships he had with certain donors who were engaged in illegal manipulation of certain corporate securities." All of this was fiction, but I figured it's untraceable and would cover me should someone ask why I'm inquiring. "I haven't alerted Trendle to this, as it's probably nothing," I add, before she can ask.

I could hear doubt creep into her voice as she says, "OK, Mark, for you I'll check it out with a couple of the old timers who were around when Trendle was a freshman member of Congress. They should know if there is anything to the rumor. Give me a few days."

SIXTEEN

A couple of days seem like forever. I decide it's time to have another conversation with Teddy at the Oil Association, so I ask one of our junior staffers to set up an appointment. Kevin, one of the new guys, comes in an hour later with a serious look on his face.

"What is it?"

"The association just called back to inform me that Theodore Edelstein was killed in an auto accident two days ago."

"What!" I say far too loudly. Shauna peeks in to see if everything is OK.

"I'm fine," I reassure her, though I'm not. As brief as our encounter had been, I just lost a friend and someone I'd hoped to spend time with engaging in the kind of spirited, intellectual dialogue I long for. On top of the tragedy of his death, it adds to the mystery swirling about me. What is this carbon conspiracy and was Al Clampton's remark simply a drunken coincidence or is it yet another clue? Suddenly, I realize Kevin is still in the office waiting for instructions.

"Thanks, and let them know how sorry I am about his death."

He nods and walks out.

Later that day, a visitor stops in and hands a thirty-page white paper to our receptionist.

"It's for Mr. Burnham."

The fact that it's hand-delivered is no surprise. Since the anthrax scare a few years back, it's impossible to mail anything and expect it to arrive in less than two weeks, if ever. Our receptionist leaves it in my in-basket. Seeing the Oil Association logo, I open it right away. My lungs suck in air as I read the handwritten note attached. It's a message from the dead.

> Mark,
>
> It was wonderful talking with you last week. I believe you may be the one person in Congress willing to consider what I shared. Someone must have noticed us together because the Oil Association director is suddenly interested in who I talked to at the conference. I don't think he was reassured when I told him we had dinner. In any case, I thought you would find the analysis I prepared interesting to read. It offers what I believe is the long-term solution to the world's need for abundant, clean, and carbon-free energy.

The note concludes with Teddy's signature scrawled at the bottom, followed by: "PS: Mark, you should ask yourself why nobody is talking about this."

I drop what I'm doing and cancel my appointments for the day. As it turned out, I would cancel the following day as well. What Teddy sent over is revolutionary, if true. The title of the paper, *Ultra Deep Geothermal Energy Production,* is nothing to rouse excitement. Anyone who advocates for green energy-production pays lip service to geothermal energy. It's a boutique source of electrical generation in a few places in the Western US and on volcanic islands. In at least one country, Iceland, it accounts for half of all energy production.

The key limitation is geological. Essentially, the generating plants need to be located near some form of volcanic or hot spring activity that brings the Earth's core heat to the surface. Wells are drilled, similar to those drilled for oil and natural gas. Once they reach a depth where the temperature is seven hundred degrees, water is piped to the bottom of the hole where it is converted to steam, which generates electricity at the plant built over the site. Virtually no carbon and no pollutants are produced in the process. Some of the newer plants send the spent steam, re-cooled to liquid, back down the hole for reheating, thus eliminating even the discharge of water vapor. Teddy acknowledged the current limitations to its widespread use in the paper; which is the reason geothermal is almost completely ignored in the discussion of fossil-free alternatives to oil. It's the second chapter that grabs my attention and causes me to sideline my schedule for the next forty-eight hours.

"Ultra-deep drilling will soon be able to reach the required seven-hundred degrees of heat in any location worldwide; thus offering the capability to eliminate all fossil-fuel-based energy production."

Is this true? And if it is, why has this not been a component of the clean energy dialogue? Clearly, my knowledge of geology and the structure of the Earth are inadequate. I need to check some facts before I read further. Remembering something, I pick up the phone and call Julie Newhouse over at the Energy Department. She's an obscure scientist in the Office of Basic Energy Sciences who served as an expert witness last year, testifying about the future state of energy production. I pull up her testimony and, sure enough, she had talked briefly about geothermal power generation.

"Julie Newhouse?"

"This is she," a cautious voice responds.

Anytime a congressional office contacts a low-level administration official, panic ensues. All that official thinks about is what she did wrong and who is being investigated. After I reassure her that this is a friendly call, she opens up.

"Julie, do you have time to talk with me about your presentation on geothermal energy at last year's hearing?"

She's silent for almost a minute, trying to recall the hearing. "Well, I kind of remember, but as I recall, we only made a passing reference to geothermal energy," she finally says.

"And that's why I called. Frankly, we are novices when it comes to geothermal energy in our office." If she thought I was calling on behalf of Trendle, so much the better. "I need someone who can educate me as to where geothermal heat comes from and how much is available. I was hoping you could provide a brief explanation."

Knowing that government employees seldom pass on free food, I offer to buy her lunch.

"That would be great," she answers quickly.

"You know how we are in Congress—always in a hurry for info. Any chance we can meet today?"

I hear the click of a keyboard. "My calendar is clear at noon."

"Great. I'll walk down to your office and meet you out front." The day is sunny and she's at headquarters on Independence Avenue, about ten blocks from where I'm sitting.

"See you at noon." With that she hangs up.

As I approach the front entrance, it's easy to spot Julie: She's the one casting about, looking for a sign of recognition.

"Julie Newhouse," I say, extending my hand.

With a relieved look, she answers, "Yes and you must be Mark Burnham."

I nod, returning the smile. Julie's in her mid-thirties, undistinguished in appearance and fashion. I'm expecting a dry discussion when she introduces the man next to her.

"Mark, I'd like you to meet Leonard Washington."

It is only then that I realize he is with her. We shake hands and make our way to a nearby weigh-the-food joint.

DC is loaded with cafeteria-type restaurants where food is purchased by the pound. After filling up our trays, we find a table in the corner where we can eat and talk.

"The real expert in our office is Leonard. He's forgotten more about the Earth's structure than most of us will ever know." Leonard smiles at that. It's obvious this guy is proud of his expertise. He's a distinguished-looking man in his early sixties with short, curly, salt-and-pepper hair, a trim mustache of similar color, and bifocals sitting on a broad nose. I suspect he's the kind of person who has no career aspirations; that the science is what turns him on. Senior department officials love guys like him because they can climb the ladder of bureaucratic success on their intellect.

"Leonard, not to be rude, but I want the Cliff Notes version of where the heat comes from for geothermal power and how much is available."

Forget the abridged version. I've found Leonard's sweet spot and for the next two hours, as I pick at my lunch, he holds my attention with an in-depth lecture of the nature of planet Earth. He's good in that I'm actually able to understand what he says. No wonder the senior people love him. Most political appointees are experts in manipulation, not science. He has the uncanny ability to make the most complex facts simple to understand.

"Think of the Earth as a fresh plum." He had actually picked one up from the food line. Carefully cutting one quarter of the plum, he continues, "Notice that this plum has three layers. Can you identify them?"

OK, he could give the Bill Nye the Science Guy a run for his money. "Sure," I reply, "The skin, the thicker fruit section, and the big pit in the center."

He nods, "Very good. The skin represents the crust of the Earth, what we are standing on. In relative terms, it is even thinner than the skin of this plum when compared to the rest of the Earth."

"So how thin is the crust?"

"It varies from five to thirty miles, and in a few places—at the sites of active volcanoes—it's no thicker than a mile or two."

"What about the pit?"

"Most scientists have concluded that the center of the Earth is a giant ball of iron mixed with nickel." Before I could ask the next question, he continues. "That, along with flowing magma provides the Earth's magnetic signature that among other things allows navigation by compass."

Makes sense, but this still doesn't explain the source of heat.

"We've left the best for last," announces Leonard, excitedly. "What we call the flesh or fruit part of the plum represents the mantle. It's a several-thousand-mile-thick, hellish environment of molten rock, approaching one thousand degrees, swirling about just below the crust." I have a feeling of déjà vu. As I was with Albert Consolvas's explanation of the history of the Earth's temperature, I'm continually reminded how one-sided my environmental education has been. It dawns on me that if our country is to make any real progress environmentally, we need to recognize how complex the situation really is.

Leonard provides a long explanation of the different gradients in the mantle and core, as well as the composition of elements contained within. I'm intrigued but decide to call a halt before my brain explodes. "Leonard, one last question, if the Earth is billions of years old, how is it still so hot inside?"

"That's an excellent question and one that has only been resolved relatively recently. Prior to the twentieth century, most scientists, including Lord Kelvin, based the age of the Earth on a static model, using the heat from volcanic lava to estimate the temperature of the interior and then extrapolating back to a time of creation much nearer than today's estimates.

"What changed was the discovery of radioactivity and the recognition that the Earth's interior is much more dynamic, with heat fueled by the decay of radioactive isotopes."

We finish up the discussion and our lunches. Thanking them profusely, I head back to the office determined to attack Teddy's paper with renewed vigor. I end up being tied up all afternoon with a surprise teleconference with Trent Watersworth from the congressman's district office. Trent periodically calls to talk about the need to pressure US Customs into backing off on its vigilant reviewing of the manifests and content of the ships and planes used to transport Malcolm Little's extensive art work. I understand the logic of supporting a major donor, but I think Trent is over the top in his passion for this issue. But as always, Trendle reluctantly agrees to bring suitable pressure on the head of the House Committee on Homeland Security.

It's not until evening, back at my apartment with left-over Chinese and a beer, that I open Teddy's document and pick up where I left off. The paper goes into detail regarding advancements in deep drilling for oil and gas. His point is that instead of bashing and taxing, extensive tax credits and other incentives should be used to encourage the majors and wildcatters to go ever deeper in search of oil and gas, especially in the lower forty-eight states. For a small investment, the US would let those drilling today continue to profit on new discoveries, especially gas, which is a step in the right direction in reducing the carbon footprint. As these wells reach the geothermal temperature threshold, they could be converted to supply unlimited, clean steam to generating plants built on site.

As I read Teddy's paper, I'm ready to abandon windmills and throw all my support behind geothermal. That is until I read the final chapter. Edelstein wasn't simply an outstanding scientist but a strategist as well, all-too-rare a combination. The final section of the paper is devoted to barriers to achieving unlimited clean energy.

It's not about the engineering challenges. The paper already makes it clear that they would be overcome as all similar past challenges have been if the incentives were properly aligned. No, what Teddy discusses are the political and financial barriers to geothermal energy independence. In this regard, the barriers are formidable and vast.

"Oil, gas, and coal have the advantage of being a commodity, which can be bought, sold, and more importantly, speculated on," Teddy writes. "Governments regularly use these resources to gain power over one another. Corporations make billions by transporting oil and gas from remote locations. They earn billions more refining and marketing it as heating oil and gasoline. Replacing all of that with the equivalent of what hydroelectric power offers today, but on a universal scale, would eliminate the inequity between countries and the need to transport energy over vast distances. One can envision neighborhoods or even single-family homes drawing heat and power from an ultra-deep well, literally at their feet."

I can't help thinking that companies such as Con-Gen would vigorously oppose a major shift to geothermal. Their investment in oil pipelines and high-voltage transmission lines would be lost. An industry built around fossil fuel would suffer the same fate as salt did. Until the nineteenth century, salt was such a scarce resource that whole cities—Venice and Amsterdam, to name two—along with a vast transportation infrastructure were built upon it. Once it became plentiful and available locally through modern mining techniques, it lost all significance. Teddy forecasts the same fate for the current financial, political, and industrial infrastructure if geothermal were to reach its full potential. He goes on to imply, without actually naming names, that powerful forces, including certain environmental concerns, are at the forefront of keeping geothermal under wraps.

Under other circumstances, I would have broached the subject with Trendle. But given recent events, I think it best to lay low until I get to the bottom of whatever is going on.

SEVENTEEN

It's been a relatively quiet week with Congress in recess and Trendle on the West Coast, spending time with his family. As I'm about to leave for the day a junior staffer walks into the office. I overhear her ask for me by name. I stick my head out the door.

"That's me. What can I do or you?"

She hands me an envelope, and before I can ask a question, she is out the door and gone. It turns out to be an invitation to an evening reception over at the Russell Senate Office Building sponsored by the Farragut North Group, with which we have nothing in common. It's a typical affair honoring members of Congress and plying them and their staffs with food and drink. This is one of many ways lobbyists legally show their love for their favorite elected officials. While I normally would not attend an event outside of our area of jurisdiction, this invitation has to be from Mabis, and so I decide to go.

As I make my way over, I immediately notice a man, a different guy this time, following me. I'm surprised at how blasé I've become about the persistent tailing. I arrive as Farragut's senior policy advisor is making opening remarks in a room crowded with staffers, business leaders, lobbyists, and a few senators. I looked around for Mabis, but she's nowhere to be found. Meanwhile, the speaker is gushing with praise for the outstanding leadership of the senators in attendance. I've heard the same nonsense speech a thousand times, but it's one that has to be made. The Farragut guy also thanks the two businesses that cosponsored the event. You can bet they are major donors of the honorees. While this is going on, staffers and lower-level attendees from the non-profits consume as much free food and drink as they can. Normally, I'd be part of the feeding frenzy, as it means one less meal I have to pay for. However, curiosity as to why Mabis wants me here keeps me focused on what's being said as I scan the room for a familiar face.

As the speeches drone on and awards are presented, I'm increasingly puzzled as to the relevancy. Perhaps I misunderstood the invitation. Or maybe she was unavoidably detained. In any case, I'm about to quietly slip out when I hear Senator Dawn Plesher, in her acceptance speech, single out Con-Gen Industries as an outstanding example of successful public-private partnership. The senior senator from Montana radiates the kind of elegant charm that makes you believe she's on your side right up until she votes against you.

This must be the connection Mabis knew I would tumble to. Another piece of the puzzle falls into place as I recall Plesher's name mentioned by Pittfield Oil's chairman during the hearing, I gave it no thought at the time figuring he was just throwing out names trying to cover his ass. Perhaps she had a hand in Edelestein's death.

The fact that she set it up this way tells me that Mabis is unwilling to stick her neck out.

I call out sick the next morning. I need to see someone about this whom I trust implicitly. I hop on the early morning Amtrak to New York and catch a cab to Columbia University, which has one of the best political science departments in the nation. A friend and mentor of mine while I was a student at Boston University is now the Wheldon C. Smith professor of political science, Chuck Wilson PhD. We've maintained a friendly relationship and connect from time to time when either of us is looking for insight from the other on some burning political issue of the moment. He's one of those rare academics who understand that theory and reality are worlds apart, especially when it comes to politics. Forewarned I'm coming, Chuck has swept clean the only other chair in his cluttered office. Now in his early fifties, he still retains that boyish enthusiasm for the seamier side of politics. For all his academic credentials, he revels in political gossip. In fact, a significant portion of his income comes from his weekly column in the *Post* blasting this governor or that senator for some sizzling indiscretion. I always marvel at his ability to dig up dirt that nine times out of ten, turns out to be true. His wiry, six-foot-two frame and academic slouch gives the impression of someone absent minded; that is until you look in his eyes and see he is wide awake and taking everything in.

"Chuck, how's the family?"

He laughs. "Complicated as always with three ex-wives, but I'm managing. How about you?"

I let him know I'm still single and my parents are well, living in the house where I grew up.

"Mark, you didn't stop by to catch up on family. What's on your mind?"

And that was that. We jump right to the business at hand. Given my reluctance to discuss it on the phone, he's especially eager to hear what he suspects are juicy details.

"Right now, what I have is out-of-character behavior from Trendle, somebody following me, and several mysterious deaths." That last statement really catches his attention.

Chuck points a finger at me. "Your political instincts are sharp as a tack. If your antennae are starting to twitch, then odds are there's something to it." He pauses and then asks, "Mark, are your sure someone is tailing you or does paranoia have you seeing something that isn't really there?"

"My tail actually pulled me back from a near hit and run and dropped a thinly veiled warning that I should mind my own business."

"I just want to be sure it's real. Did you notice anything unusual about this particular guy?"

"It didn't seem significant at the time but he definitely had an accent."

"Could you identify what kind?

"It's hard to say. Maybe Central or South American."

Thinking for a moment, Chuck says, "That could be significant. But for the moment, let's put the identity of your shadow on hold. Start from the beginning."

I proceed to lay it out for him: The phony credit scare, Trendle's odd remark questioning global warming, my outreach to Mabis, tracking my calls, the unexplained connection of Senator Plesher to Con-Gen Industries, and the substance of the discussion I had with Teddy Edelstein. When I come to the part about the carbon conspiracy, he raises his eyebrows and jots those words on a sheet of paper. When I finish, Chuck leans back in his chair with hands folded, silently digesting it all.

Finally, he asks, "Is that it?"

I hand over Edelstein's paper and suggest he read it through. Skipping quickly through the technical portions, he slows up and carefully studies the last section regarding political barriers.

"Your friend Teddy is a surprise. I'd love to talk to him."

He notes the grim expression on my face. "What is it?

"Unfortunately, Teddy was killed last week in an accident."

Chuck stares at the floor as one does when a loss is discussed.

"You said deaths…," he says, finally looking up.

I brief him on Connie Imlen's paper, which was submitted without the knowledge of her employer, TCC Industries, and her subsequent death along with the abnormal interest

Trendle gave to the existence of the paper, his warning to back off, and the interrogation I received from Trent.

I was unprepared for what comes out of Chuck's mouth next. "Mark, this is serious stuff. You're in deep water here and need to be very careful. It's a matter of life and death."

He looks me in the eye and points a finger, "Yours."

"Come on, there's got to be—"

He cuts me off mid-sentence. "Give me a few days to look into this. It may confirm a rumor I picked up from another source."

I push him for further details but all he will say is to be careful and to watch my back. As I get up to leave, he advises me to lay low and do nothing until I hear from him. With a sharp look, he adds, "And don't tell anyone about our discussion."

Thoroughly mystified and more concerned than ever, I ride the evening train back to DC lost in thought. Why is Chuck being so secretive? I recall the hint of fear in his voice as he spoke and wonder if it was concern for himself, me, or someone else. Now I'm really scared. Chuck's seldom wrong when it comes to political intrigue. He loves gossip and files every bit of it in that steel-trap mind of his to be recalled at some future time to point out an inconsistency or simply make some politician's life miserable in his biting op-eds that the *Post* loves to print. One of the reasons I've never told Trendle about Chuck is that he has more than once embarrassed Trendle. As the Acela speeds through the Maryland flatlands, I decide to let this sleeping dog lie until I hear back from Chuck.

As soon as I walk into my apartment, my cell vibrates. It's Shauna informing the staff that Trendle wants everyone in the office at 6:00 a.m. All hell has broken loose over a major oil spill off the Florida Keys.

EIGHTEEN

Trendle bursts in a few minutes after six, coffee in hand, ready to rumble. "Mark, I demand a hearing on this oil spill fiasco. Get it scheduled ASAP." He's wired and ready to lynch every oil executive between DC and the Gulf of Mexico.

"Shauna," he yells, "call a press conference. Those clowns from *The Wall Street Journal* better be there." He hates the *Journal*. Its stories are intelligent, logical, and in his estimation, are totally biased in favor of big profits over progress. Of course *The Wall Street Journal* will be there and of course the next morning Trendle will be cursing it up, down, and sideways after reading the inevitable editorial ripping his left-wing politics. Trendle and the *Journal* are like a long-married, bickering couple ever threatening divorce but never going through with it.

The press conference is masterful. Trendle's statement, which I authored, paints Pittfield Oil, the perpetrator of the spill, as the enemy of big business. Because of the company's gross (I convinced Trendle not to use "criminal" just yet) negligence, prime vacation property and the Caribbean cruise industry are in jeopardy. Trendle goes on to say that Pittfield is dragging down the good name of those oil companies that truly care about the environment. In fact, Trendle never met an oil company he didn't hate and would never believe that any of them cares about the environment. But pitting oil against oil makes for great press coverage and becomes the topic of several of CNN's *Situation Room* reports. All of this is warm-up for the hearing, Trendle's number one weapon of choice. He has the entire staff researching every environmental incident on file or in the press for the last twenty years related to Pittfield. We even find an old news clip in which a much younger Win Chalmers, founder and chairman of Pittfield, is asked about the danger oil imposes to the environment. He sarcastically responds, "I don't give a shit about a few dead dolphins and seagulls coated in oil."

In baseball terminology, if the New Jersey spill was a single, this one could prove to be the grand slam homerun Trendle's been looking for. He knows that if Key West is destroyed, or even severely compromised, the oil companies can look forward to a hundred years of litigation from which they may never recover. If that happens, the urgency for wind and other renewable energy will unleash the biggest government-sponsored development program since the building of the Hoover Dam.

We're looking for weaknesses to exploit. With Chalmers, it quickly becomes apparent we have lots to work with. He's hotheaded and ruthless. His much-publicized four marriages, frequent clashes with the press, and reputation as a take-no-prisoners negotiator means he has many enemies. Guys like him always seem invincible until you find their Achilles heels. And we found it. Over the years, he built strong ties with the congressional delegation from Texas. In particular House Minority Leader, Jim Greentree provides lots of political cover for Chalmers, who, in turn, keeps him flush with campaign funds. It turns out that Chalmers and Greentree have been on the outs since Chalmers divorced his third wife, Greentree's daughter, for an even younger beauty queen. Without Greentree's protection, Pittfield Oil is vulnerable.

The plan is to arrange for Pittfield to be hit with a series of safety inquiries encouraged by Congress. Normally, the safety regulations are routinely ignored—or rather, they are minimally followed. It's as much the company's fault as that of the workers themselves who cut corners to bring the oil fields in on schedule and boost their own bonuses. Whenever there is a serious injury or death, the victim and his family are heavily compensated in return for agreeing to forego civil litigation. A full-blown Occupational Safety and Health Administration (OSHA) procedural audit would force the companies to enforce the safety regulations fully, thus slowing the pace of the drilling to a near standstill.

That's where we launch our attack. Trendle summons OSHA Inspector General Matt Grogan to his office for a quiet conversation about how disappointed he is that the serious injuries in the Brantana oil field in western Montana are well above acceptable levels. Trendle and the IG know that the number of injuries is always high in new and active fields, and Brantana is particularly robust. Even more important, it's Pittfield's most promising and profitable new field. The stars are in alignment. We have the golden opportunity to put Big Oil on the ropes. By bringing Pittfield Oil to its knees, we'll send a clear message to the entire industry: play ball and support renewable energy or go the way of tobacco with endless litigation, ever-increasing regulation, and punitive taxes. I'm flying high. All else is forgotten as Trendle drives us mercilessly in preparation for a hearing targeting Pittfiels's safety record.

I'm on cloud nine in anticipation of scoring a major victory in the ongoing struggle to preserve the planet. But at one time or another, we idealistic, high-energy, very bright insiders all are hijacked by our own political propaganda. I'd forgotten that our system of government is designed with checks and balances, and has political parties and thousands of voices all competing for their special interest and protecting their turf. I even forget that grandfathering is a necessary ingredient for stability and gradual transition from the known to something new.

And so it happens quietly. For a while, I didn't notice—or rather, chose to ignore—the invisible yet very real waves of influence, bureaucracy, and indifference that began to soften and blunt the sharp edge of our attack.

Two days before the press conference, Trendle pops his head into my office. "Mark, lets hold off briefing the press about the hearing. Greentree seems to have gotten over his daughter's heartbreak and wants to know why we are going after his man."

I'm stunned. "Why? The time is ripe. We have Pittfield right where we want it."

"Not to worry," Trendle cheerfully replies. "Just need a few days to settle Greentree down."

And that was it. Trendle was off to some party caucus related to a freshman congressman's indiscretion with one of the pages. The energy drains out of my body and is replaced by a feeling of intense frustration. When one is running the race flat out and the victory line is in sight, the smallest obstacle seems catastrophic. So it is with this. Furthermore, with Greentree back in the game, our opportunity is slipping away. Delays in and of themselves are a major problem. After a few days, the press will start to lose interest and begin to look for the next crisis. Once that happens, it is very difficult to regain its attention.

I'm utterly exhausted and depressed when I leave the office for the night. I decide to walk toward the Washington Monument. The one piece of good news is that since meeting with Chuck, I'm no longer being tailed. At least not that I notice. Perhaps they've finally lost interest in me.

It always comforts me to know that if George Washington could handle Valley Forge, then I can handle any problems that come my way. As I reach the reflecting pool, my cell phone vibrates. It's Chuck.

"Mark, I have to make this quick." He sounds very anxious, as if someone is listening in. "When can you get to New York? I found something very big that involves Trendle."

I push hard for details but all he will say is that it involves his early years and family connections.

"I'll fill you in when you get here. I need to run this by somebody who might be able to provide the big picture."

It's Wednesday and I promise Chuck I'll come up by the weekend.

Friday arrives and I'm on the exercise bike at 6:50 a.m. when CNN breaks in with a special report. "Charles Wilson, noted professor of political science at Columbia University, found dead in his apartment; an apparent victim of suicide."

I nearly fall off the bike. I stumble out of the gym, stunned. I find a wall and collapse against it. A couple of staffers I know poke their heads out the door to ask if I'm OK. I wave them off, unable to verbalize the grief I feel. It doesn't seem possible that Chuck is dead. Perhaps they made a mistake. Yet I know they haven't. The more I ponder the news, the more I'm convinced it's related to what Chuck wouldn't tell me over the phone. I quickly dress and show up at the office long enough to announce I'm taking a few days off due to the death of a friend.

Trendle isn't in town. I'm relieved. My suspicion that Trendle and Chuck's death are connected is a real possibility, but I'm not prepared to confront him at this time.

Catching the midday train to New York, I arrive at Chuck's apartment by 4:30 p.m. The crime scene tape is still up, though Chuck's body has been removed. As I look in, there sitting on the sofa is an attractive woman in her twenties, being interviewed by a detective. I recognize her as Chuck's niece, Emily, whom I've met a couple of times over the years. Linda Snow, Emily's mom, was widowed young when her Marine husband was killed by an IED. With Emily to care for, she relied heavily on Chuck, who was glad to serve as the surrogate male influence in Emily's life. That relationship became even more important after her Mom died of cancer two years ago.

"Emily, it's Mark." The police approach quickly, ready to haul me off. Fortunately, she recognizes me before they can.

"Detective, it's OK. Mark is one of my uncle's dearest friends." She forces a smile but I can see she's close to losing it.

"Detective, is there any chance Emily can finish her statement later?" I ask. "She needs to rest."

"I'm about done anyway. I'll send someone around tomorrow if we need any additional information."

With that, he's out the door.

I sit down next to her and take her hand in mine. Her slender frame shakes violently as she cries on my shoulder. It's obvious she needs this, so we sit for almost an hour without saying a word. Finally, out of sheer exhaustion, she falls into a restless sleep. Emily's grief is helping me deal with my own. After carrying Emily to the spare bedroom, I crash on the couch. Sleeping in or even entering Chuck's bedroom would not have been possible for either of us.

I awake to the aroma of fresh-brewed coffee and realize its early Saturday morning. She's calmer now but the grief is still evident in the slowness of her movements. As we drink coffee, I ask her what happened. She stares at the table and with a pleading look in her eyes says, "Mark, there is no way Uncle Charles committed suicide. He loved life too much and he never took drugs."

She sees the look of surprise on my face. Given his free-wheeling lifestyle and periodic bursts of explosive emotion, many of us assumed he did drugs; at least smoked pot once in a while. When I mention this to her she responds, "Lots of people thought that but it simply wasn't true. He was a fanatic about never using drugs. He even avoided prescription antibiotics, if at all possible. He would often lecture me, saying, 'I've seen too many of my students and colleagues with promising futures shipwreck their lives on drugs.' Don't get me wrong. He was a fun-loving guy who loved to debate any political issue while downing a few beers."

I nod and smile, remembering how after some particularly intense and stimulating discussion, he would say, "Let's continue this at The Dugout," a local pub favored by BU students. We'd gather over burgers and pitchers of beer and argue our respective positions until closing.

We fell silent, each caught up in our own memories of better times, trying with little success to banish the gloom. Finally dragging myself back to the present, I knew I needed to ask her something.

"Emily, was there anything bothering your uncle?"

Immediately getting defensive, she retorts, "Why do you ask? You sound like that detective who was interviewing me." Her emotions start to boil over again. "I told that detective and I'm telling you now there was nothing going on that would have led him to take his own life." Tears are streaming down her face as she speaks.

I hold up my hand and apologize. "That isn't what I meant. It seems inconceivable to me as well." I stop and look into her red-rimmed eyes, trying to gauge if I should go on. Her expression says yes. "The reason I'm asking is because a few weeks ago I came to New York to see Chuck and asked him to do some research related to Congressman Trendle." It's obvious she knows nothing about this, so I quickly fill her in.

"I contacted him a few weeks ago because I wanted his opinion regarding some political issues I'm wrestling with in Congress." I decide not to share my own fears or the anxiety in Chuck's voice when he phoned me the other day. "He called me a few days after our meeting and indicated he'd found something important and needed to take a deeper look."

Emily is thoughtful for a few minutes and then, much calmer, she says, "Come to think of it, my uncle was clearly engaged in some kind of hot research. I called the other day to let him know I was coming to New York to attend a legal conference."

As it turns out, Emily Snow is a promising young attorney specializing in international law.

"He declined to meet me, which was unusual for him. He said he was in the middle of some very important research. Uncle Charles was all excited. He remarked that this was his ticket to a political expose even better than Deep Throat."

We fall silent again as I ponder this new piece of information. I'm careful to keep any concern off my face, but inside I'm filled with turmoil. My mind is racing. What did Chuck find that's so controversial? Worse, could I have been the cause of his death? While logic dictates there is nothing to feel guilty about, friendship and my own involvement makes that unrealistic. It's deeply personal. The only way to assuage the guilt is to get to the bottom of it.

"Emily, the coroner will conduct an autopsy. I strongly recommend you hire a private medical examiner to participate."

With a scared expression, she promises to do so.

"I'll give you a call next week to see how you're doing."

With a brief hug, I leave the apartment and begin to walk downtown toward Times Square. I need time to think, to try to make sense of it all. I've been mixing it up long enough with politicians and their behind-the-scenes maneuvering that I quickly dismiss the notion that this could have been a horrible coincidence. His death has to be related to the research in which we were engaged. It no longer seems plausible that Teddy's death was an accident. Now I have two deaths weighing heavily on my conscience. They must be connected to the unexplained accident that took the life of Connie Imlen.

On top of it all, there's something else on my mind and it catches me by surprise. I realize that Emily is not simply Chuck's niece but an attractive woman sharing her sorrow and fears with me. This leaves me with a lingering desire to get to know her better. I quickly force this thought out of my conscious. A romantic entanglement is the last thing I need right now.

NINETEEN

I wake up exhausted the next morning. The events of the last few weeks kept playing over and over in my thoughts all night. I still can't believe Chuck is gone. How did things get so crazy? It all began with my digging into Connie Imlen's paper. Each revelation has fueled my suspicions and suggests darker secrets remain to be found. Trendle's offhand remark, Connie Imlen and Edelstein's deaths, and the hint of something sinister in the references to a carbon conspiracy are troubling in and of themselves. Adding to the mystery is the devious way Mabis maneuvered me to the reception where the connection between Senator Dawn Plesher, a complete unknown to me, and Con-Gen was revealed. Now, a week after sharing these things with Chuck, he's dead.

His warning to lay low still rings in my ears. It doesn't add up. There has to be a missing link somewhere and I'm determined to find it. Three questions loom large. What else does Mabis know, what is Con-Gen's connection to Plesher, and where does Edelstein fit in?

Before heading back to DC, I decide to see if I can get into Chuck's office on campus to poke around for clues. When I was his student at BU, he had a habit of leaving his key under the fire extinguisher in the hallway outside the office. Only a few of his favorite students knew about this and I wondered if he continued the practice at Columbia. It was a "privilege" being on the inside with Professor Chuck, as we called him, thus we jealously guarded this information. I used to pop into his office after closing when I was deep into research on a paper he'd assigned. Whenever he found me next morning, usually asleep with my head on the desk, he'd put on coffee and pepper me with questions about the position I'd taken and try to poke holes in my arguments. He was a master of the Socratic Method.

Step one is getting on campus. Security is tougher in the post 9-11 world but campuses being what they are, it is possible to circumvent the sleepy guards. As always, the key to foiling any security system is to look like you belong. I catch the subway down to Union Square and cruise a few clothing shops until I have the appropriately broken in jeans, canvas sneakers, and a T-shirt with Che Guevara's bearded picture on the back. I check into a cheap hotel, change out of my suit, and spend fifteen minutes in front of the mirror doing my best to completely mess up my hair. While I can't pass for an undergraduate, there are many PhD candidates in their late twenties and early thirties, which is the look I'm going for.

The other key to penetrating security is to act impatient and in a hurry to get something on campus related to an event that security knows about. I browse the Columbia website on my smartphone for events that evening. As luck would have it, the Black Box Theatre on campus is hosting yet another experimental production of Ben Jonson's *Volpone*. This version, entitled, *Screw You Before You Screw Me*, is directed by a Professor Kenneth Seldon. I print out the title page and scoop up some papers left in the printer and staple the title on top.

I catch the subway uptown and start walking by Columbia's various entrances until I spot an appropriately young and clearly bored security guard. Twenty minutes before the curtain goes up, I start running about a block from the entrance and arrive out of breath and looking panic-stricken. Script in hand, I stop to catch my breath "Hey man, I need to get this script to Professor Seldon right away," I say, as I flash the pages in front of him, knowing he won't bother to look.

In a bored voice he replies, "ID."

"Hold this." I hand him the script and start rummaging through my pockets. After a minute of searching, I started cursing. "Oh shit, I left my ID in the room. I need to get this to the professor before the play begins. There are some script changes." I continue whining, "He is going to flunk me for sure."

He stares at me for a moment and looks around to see if anyone's nearby. "OK, I'm not supposed to do this. Just show me some sort of ID." I fish my Library of Congress card out of my back pocket. A wallet would have looked out place for a theater major. As I flash the library card, I ramble on about my thesis on avant-garde theater in Colonial America. With that, he waves me through. I thank him and promise not to tell anyone he let me through without an ID card. I make my way quickly through the gate, ensuring it's too late for him to change his mind.

Upon reaching the poli-sci building, I go around back, hop up on the loading dock, grab a bundle of toilet paper, and wait for one of the cleaning people to open the door. Sure enough, after a few minutes, a middle-aged Hispanic woman in a housekeeping uniform opens the door and walks out pushing a loaded trash bin. Seeing I have the paper, she barely gives me a look as I stroll through the open door and race up the stairs. Chuck's office is on the third floor. As I enter the hallway, there's a fire extinguisher. Sure enough, the key is under it. Letting myself in, I immediately sit down in front of his desktop computer and begin to scan the cluttered office, wondering where to begin. Thank God, Emily has not yet come by to clean out the office.

"What is going on?" I keep asking myself, feeling guilty over his death. Surfing his computer would take too much time and with the number of student hackers trying to steal and sell exams, most professors heavily protect their computers. They seldom keep sensitive material on the hard drive.

Focusing on the task before me, I realize the challenge is figuring out where to look. I'm not worried about fingerprints, since I was here just last week. Besides, the police undoubtedly took a quick look already, and they believe it's a suicide.

I don't want to spend hours tearing the office apart, as there's still the risk the night watchman will catch me. I let my eyes run over the stacks of papers that are everywhere and then to the much neglected bookshelf in the corner. I notice a Bible among the political books and journals. That reminds me of a quirky habit Chuck had. Whenever he was engaged in deep background research, he would make cryptic notes on yellow Post-its and put them under scripture passages in an old Bible he had. I asked him about it once.

"Mark, I don't know whether God is real or invented to explain the unexplainable, but the Bible is filled with scandal and intrigue. It's a great resource about the inner workings of the human psyche."

It's a well-worn Gideon's Bible, and looks like the same one he had during my undergraduate days. Sure enough, as I thumb through it, I find various scattered notes with initials on them. "TT" I figure represents Trendle. "CS" possibly stands for carbon scandal or maybe Chet Southers. A couple of others do not ring a bell. I continue leafing through the pages, and there in the book of Leviticus, in Chapter 16, right next to the description of the scapegoat, is a piece of paper with my initials, MB, written on it. My mouth goes dry and my heart starts to pound. That explains why he warned me to be careful. The biblical message is clear. I've opened a can of worms and could end up becoming the fall guy. But who is behind all this and why?

My thoughts are interrupted by a noise down the hall. I turn out the lights and peek out. The security guard is opening each office and stepping in to take a look. Having no time to copy or write the information down, I simply grab the Bible and when the guard steps into the next office, I slip out. I make my way down the back stairs and out of the building, making sure to leave the campus via a different route than when I came in.

For the entire train ride home, I obsess over the scapegoat connection. Chuck did not pick these passages lightly. It's only when I'm back in DC and in my apartment that I have the time to study the verses in detail. The reference is clear. The scapegoat takes on the sins of the people and is then banished. Chuck thought some great evil was swirling about me and if it became known, the blame would be laid on my shoulders. Somehow, this is all connected with Trendle. But how?

This has turned into a nightmare. Normally, I'm the one in charge and on the offensive. Always being in command of the facts has given me the upper hand. The inevitable political battles on the Hill reinforce my can-do, take-no-prisoners attitude. The adrenaline high from such battles is intoxicating.

Within a matter of a week, I've found myself out of my element, fearful, filled with grief, and quite alone. Whom can I turn to with Chuck gone? In other circumstances, I might reach out to Mabis, but she clearly isn't willing to stick her neck out. Perhaps Teddy held the key to this, but he, too, is dead.

On Monday morning, Trendle pops into my office and offers his condolences over Chuck's death. I thank him and decide it's best to pitch a cover story about my visit a week earlier. By bringing it up before he asks, I hope this will allay any suspicion on Trendle's part.

"I can't believe it," I say. "Only last week I visited Chuck and asked him to do some digging into rumors related to the Pittfield oil spill and the comments I overheard from staffers suggesting you benefited politically by attacking the oil industry."

I notice Trendle visibly relax, which further fuels my suspicion regarding his role in Chuck's death. "Mark, there's a lot of jealousy over the environmental progress I've made. A few staffers' caustic remarks are nothing to worry about."

The rest of the week is taken up with the normal business of Congress, so it's not until the weekend that I have time to open Chuck's Bible and study the other quotes and references in some detail. The TT reference talks about the sins of the father flowing down to the fourth generation. What evil of Trendle's could Chuck possibly be referring to that spans generations? Yes, he's a skilled and at times ruthless politician, but he is always focused on the greater good. How can anyone argue that a clean environment is not wholesome? Trendle is the pied piper, tirelessly working to drag a kicking-and-screaming Congress away from the obvious harm that fossil fuel produces and toward a cleaner environment powered by renewable energy.

The initials "CS" were circled and placed under the passage where Joseph, second youngest son of Jacob, is set up by Potiphar's wife to cover her own indiscretion after he is sold into Egyptian slavery. Perhaps my discussions with Chet Southers have become known but how the Bible story relates is not clear. After spending most of Saturday unsuccessfully trying to decipher the meaning of all this, I decide to walk down to Trinity's, just south of the Cannon office building on First Street, for a couple of beers. It's a favorite bar of House staffers who live in the area.

While I'm nursing my second brew, a guy sits down to my left and interrupts my thoughts.

"Excuse me, could you pass the nuts?"

As I grab the bowl and turn to hand it to him, he says, "Hey, don't I know you?"

With a blank look, I shake my head. "Not that I recall."

Since I'm alone and idle chitchat is always a good way to banish dark thoughts, I decide to engage. "Most of us who frequent this place are House staffers. You work on the Hill?"

"Sure, I'm chief of staff for Senator Plesher."

A light goes on. "I remember you from a recent reception I attended over at Russell." Not yet suspicious, only curious, I'm surprised this guy is here. House staffers are a cliquey group, as are our counterparts in the Senate, and we tend not to mix socially.

"I'm Steve Landsworth," he says, putting out his hand. "The senator and I were surprised to see you at the reception."

OK, now I'm suspicious. This guy didn't just happen to be here. He was looking for me.

"You must have been lost, wandering over to the Senate."

Given the recent events, I've become cautious in what I say. So I keep it light and force a laugh. "Trendle suggested I stop by since one of our corporate supporters was being honored. It's always good to show the love."

I'm not sure if the explanation satisfies him, but he lets it drop. Since March Madness is down to the final four, we discuss the college rankings and defend our respective favorites, Florida State for me and UCLA for him. After twenty minutes of this, Steve rises from the bar stool and shakes my hand.

"Nice to meet you. Next time you're over our way, stop by." With that, he's out the door.

Something else to ponder, I'm seeing conspiracy in every encounter and every conversation. Perhaps it's paranoia. I can't tell at this point, but I decide to opt for looking over my shoulder. I spend the rest of the weekend puttering around the apartment with ESPN on in the background. Sunday is the one day staffers look forward to having some quiet time, at least until late afternoon when e-mail traffic picks up. In spite of the hours of college basketball and mindless commentary from the sportscasters, I'm unable to relax. I keep replaying the events of recent days, trying to make sense of it all. A growing sense of anger replaces my grief over Chuck's death. The weekend would have been a complete bust but for a phone call that turned out to be a welcome distraction.

"Hello, is this Mark?" a voice asks.

"Yes, what can I do for you?" I reply, slightly annoyed.

The caller at the other end picks up on this. "I'm sorry to disturb you. Would it be better if I called you at the office?"

At this point, it's too late anyway and since she's apologetic, my attitude softens. "No problem. Go ahead."

"I don't know if you remember me. We met at a West Coast reception. I'm Chloe Sullivan, Lucas Davidson's attorney of assignment." Suddenly, I don't mind taking a Sunday morning call.

"Of course I remember. It's great to hear from you." There's nothing like a call from a beautiful woman to brighten one's outlook.

"I'll be in town this week representing the firm on some important but terribly boring business before the Supreme Court."

I'll bet it's boring. Given her relationship with Justice Kensington, her mere presence at the plaintiff's table will ensure that he pays attention. But fleeting thoughts of judicial conquest quickly evaporate with her next words.

"I'm wondering if you would like to get together for dinner."

Given all that has transpired, it sounds like a great idea. Especially since the invitation comes out of the blue. We agree to meet at Boudreaux's in Georgetown—good food, quiet atmosphere, and lots of privacy where we can talk. We decide on Wednesday evening.

Fortunately, Hill work over the next three days is extremely busy. We're fine-tuning an amendment to a larger tax bill. This keeps my anticipation in check. The amendment itself offers tax credits to farmers who host windmills on their property. Trendle's strategy is to introduce the amendment during morning business rather than in the

Finance Committee, since he's not a member. This will, of course, immediately piss off the chairman of Finance big time, and he subsequently will call Trendle to ream him out, which is the whole point anyway. Once Trendle calms him down, he'll offer some legislative favor that convinces the chairman to agree to add the language during markup.

TWENTY

Wednesday evening rolls around and I find myself at the bar in Boudreaux's a half hour early, sipping a Miller Light. At the appointed time, a gentle hand rests on my shoulder and familiar voice says, "Hello Mark."

A jolt like an electric shock passes through me as I turn, take Chloe's hand in mine, and invite her to sit down. She looks great—even prettier than I remember—and is just as engaging. She sips a drink as we talk about everything and nothing for a good hour. Finally, we move to a quiet booth, order dinner, and continue talking. Chloe is vivacious and clearly as interested in me as I am in her. We connect on so many levels—political leanings, sports, and shared environmental views—that it feels like I've found my soul mate.

"Mark, it was so terrible about that Professor at Columbia University who was found dead last week?"

She caught me off guard but the expression on her face made me realize she was just making conversation.

"I knew him" I said dryly.

She obviously notes the tension in my voice. "I'm so sorry I had no idea."

"How could you know. I'm still in a bit of shock," I say. "Chuck is—was a good friend. He was a mentor of mine at BU and we became close. Shortly after I took the job with Trendle, he accepted a professorship at Columbia University. I often consulted Chuck on legislative issues. His instinct regarding the political mood of the voters was superb."

"How did he die?"

"It's been ruled a suicide by the police."

She says nothing and I continue.

As much for Chloe's protection as my own, I decide to stick with the story I told Trendle. "That's what's so sad and frustrating. Chuck was fun-loving and so full of life that I just can't believe it. The police asked me about his use of alcohol and drugs."

Actually, they had asked Emily this, but its best not to involve her even though I so want to tell Chloe the whole story. As we talk, she slips onto the banquette next to me and places her hand on mine. Her obvious sympathy for the pain I feel soothes the hurt inside.

As the evening draws to a close, I'm tempted to ask her to spend the night. Given the warmth and intimacy of the evening, there's hope that Chloe will say yes. However, while

I'm not particularly prudish, I have an aversion to random bedding of women. Call me old fashioned, but that's how I see it. I walk her out and hail a taxi. She put her arms around me and we part with a long, passionate kiss. The warmth of her lips communicates that she, too, wants our relationship to continue.

The next morning, still aglow from the previous evening, I'm jarred out of my reverie by a summons to fly out to the West Coast for an ad hoc briefing of the WW9 regarding the latest progress in the war to save the planet. This request from the Wise and Wealthy Nine is unusual in that my next scheduled visit is just a week away. But it's happened before, especially when their collective egos needed stroking.

The airline has me crammed in a middle seat in the last row. Evidence that this trip is going to be anything but routine begins on the flight. On my right, I'm cursed with an overweight salesman who lacks the ability to fly in silence. He insists on introducing himself. "Jack Matthews," he says, sticking out his hand. "I'm a wholesale distributer of wallpaper."

Forced to acknowledge his presence, I shake his hand as the smells of whiskey and stale cigarettes assault my senses. "Nice to meet you," I say unenthusiastically and quickly turn my attention to a paperback. I'm hoping he'll take the hint and lose interest, but no such luck.

"Wallpaper is a lot more complicated than people think. The artist has to design new patterns every year and then I have to convince the local retailers that they'll sell like hotcakes." I'm forced to sit through a thirty-minute lecture on why wallpaper is superior to paint and the stuff coming from China is killing the American economy.

"What line of work are you in?"

"I'm a congressional staffer."

"I hope you don't work for one of those liberal congressmen. They're always trying to screw business. They've heaped so many regs on manufacturers, it's no wonder they've moved all the work overseas. Hell, a little pollution doesn't hurt anyone. So what congressman do you work for?"

When I say Trendle, I think he'll blow a gasket. He rants for another ten minutes, making it clear that Trendle is public enemy number one. I do manage to discover that he's heading back to his hometown of Fairbanks, Alaska. This explains his friendly curiosity. I spent a week there a few years back and quickly discovered that once the locals discover you're a stranger, they pepper you with questions about every facet of your life.

I launch into an impassioned defense of our position. For being so drunk, he listens attentively and without interruption to my little speech. When I finish, he gives me a knowing look, winks, and says, "It's all a conspiracy, isn't it?"

I nearly fly out of my seat. "Listen pal, in a few years you'll be on your knees thanking Congressman Trendle for saving this country from self-destruction," I say, highly incensed. Who does this drunk think he is, anyway? "All you care about up there is lining your pockets with oil profits while destroying the environment in the process."

"Better than the Washington politicos stealing our hard-earned money," he retorts. "All your man and the rest of his kind want is to create a giant bureaucracy that sucks every dollar out of my pocket. They're in cahoots with Wall Street and foreigners to break this country's spirit."

Who these conspirators are I'm unable to discover. Teddy, Clampton, and now this guy talking about conspiracies can't be a coincidence. With security tight on airplanes these days, I'm forced to restrain myself from browbeating the truth out of him.

He's far cleverer than he seems. Thirty minutes before landing, he summons the flight attendant and asks if he can deplane ahead of the rest of us. He tells her he needs to make his connection to Fairbanks, as his mother has only a few hours to live. Having spent the past five hours with this guy, I know that's pure fiction. But the attendant is all sympathy. He's off the flight and long gone by the time I deplane. Thinking about how cleverly he baited me with that conspiracy remark, I suspect this guy was sent by someone to warn me, threaten me, inform me, or find out what I know. The scary part is not knowing which of those theories is true.

The limo drops me in the driveway. As I approach, the magnificent, ten-foot, oak, brass, and glass doors open to reveal Liddy, drink in hand, waiting to greet me. She immediately leads me back to the pool. "Mark, how about a gin and tonic?"

"Sure." I'm initially taken aback, as this is so out of character. Usually I'm working the phones with Trendle and his district office manager, Trent, right up to the start of the evening session. But the sun is out, the temperature hot, and the view, including Liddy in very revealing swimwear, is magnificent.

Wallpaper guy is still on my mind, but gin with Liddy manages to back-burner that concern for the moment.

"Mark, darling, how's your love life these days?"

I tell her about Chloe's presence in Washington. "In fact, we met up for dinner last evening. I have to thank you for introducing us. Chloe is really a wonderful person."

She nods and smiles. "I'd thought you'd find her interesting. Did you—?"

Before she can complete the thought, I say, "Liddy, I don't kiss and tell."

She is satisfied that her matchmaking is a success and we spend the rest of the afternoon discussing several pet projects of hers. By the time evening arrives, I'm relaxed and thoroughly enjoying myself.

The meeting with the WW9, itself unusual in that all nine are present, is another matter. I'm the only guest and dinner is more formal than usual. We eat in silence, a situation designed to make one uncomfortable. The somber expressions of those at the table do nothing to ease my discomfort. As we're finishing dessert, Betty Preston, the oldest of the Rumple Sisters, speaks up. "Mark, we need to understand your disloyalty."

This is a double shock to the system. Not only am I taken aback by that aggressive statement, I'm even more surprised that it's comes from Betty. I can't recall the Rumple Sisters ever taking charge of a conversation. With my thoughts racing a mile a minute, I need to make a decision about what to say and what to withhold within a matter of seconds. Finally unable to stall any further, I say, "Miss Preston I have never been disloyal and have always tried to provide you with accurate information."

It still doesn't click until T.C. intervenes. "We want to know what your meeting with Professor Wilson entailed." Again, I need to make a quick judgment as to what I can share with this group. While the members of the WW9 are a mainstay of Trendle's support, I've never really trusted them. They're too circumspect, in love with their own self-importance, and on the surface at least an odd collection of individuals. Since its unclear how much they know there's no sense in lying. I decide the best defense is a vigorous offense.

"I'm surprised you know or even care about the meeting. Chuck Wilson is…er…was an old friend and mentor. I've consulted with him over the years on all sorts of political issues. A couple of weeks back, I overheard a conversation among staffers questioning Trendle's environmental commitment."

T.C. jumps in. "So what? He's a politician and criticism is a way of life."

"True, but I've seen good men burned over the years by spurious comments morphing to serious opposition. Meeting with Chuck gave me an opportunity to see if he had heard anything that we should be concerned about. Most of the time, these inquiries turn out to be nothing. And that was the case with this visit as well."

The expressions on their faces tell me they're trying to decide if I'm telling the truth.

"Did the professor discover anything at all?" Malcolm Little purrs. This guy scares me more than any of the others.

I need to tread cautiously. Without actually lying, I reply, "I talked with him maybe a week later and he had nothing to report. Next thing I know he's dead."

They can hear the pain in my voice, which I do nothing to hide.

Liddy ends the inquisition. "Oh, Mark, please accept our apology for these rude questions." She takes my hand as she says this. "We heard rumors about your meeting with Professor Wilson and we know he is not a friend of most politicians. As you know, we are very fond of Congressman Trendle and you. We were deeply worried that you may be in some kind of trouble."

I silently shake my head in a manner conveying sadness over the topic and hurt that they're questioning my integrity. They seem satisfied with the explanation. Yet an alarm bell goes off in my head. How did they even know I was talking with Chuck? And of greater concern, who is the source of their intelligence?

The one person who could have tipped them off is Mabis. But I can't believe it. She's one of the few people on the Hill I trust. With that said, they're certainly running scared about something related to my inquiry. What have I gotten myself into? I guess my continued look of puzzlement convinces most of the WW9 that I'm innocent, since they continue to mumble apologies. Dinner finally ends and Liddy walks me out, all warmth and sympathy. Only the matriarch, Betty, retains a visible look of suspicion.

As I look back, I catch site of Betty and Malcolm deep in conversation over some point of contention between them.

On the flight back to DC, I thankfully have a row to myself. I make a decision to get to the bottom of this, beginning by identifying who the source of the leak is. My career and reputation are at risk.

I'm not looking forward to the difficult conversation with Trendle I know is awaiting me. Sure enough, as soon as I walk in, Trendle summons me to his office.

"Mark, I'm extremely disappointed in you," he barks at me. "Why would you consult with someone you and I both know is no friend of Congress members?" Before I can open my mouth to remind him I'd already discussed Chuck with him, he continues, "And why was I not aware that you were meeting about me?"

He glares at me with a mixture of anger and suspicion. Obviously, my earlier explanation was not satisfactory. It's likely he had initiated the inquisition by the WW9.

I respond with the same message I offered the WW9, as they'll undoubtedly compare notes with Trendle.

"Congressman, there are several persons I've stayed in touch with over the years. From time to time, I consult them when tracking down a rumor or doing some damage control." I go on to relate the rest of the story I'd fed the WW9.

After listening to the explanation, Trendle simply says, "Don't let it happen again. I need you on the team."

That was it. Our relationship picked up where it had always been. By the end of the week, I conclude that whatever Trendle's involvement may be, he's not the spy.

TWENTY-ONE

On the surface, the business of Congress returns to normal. I continue to handle key meetings with influential lobbyists, environmental groups, business leaders, and local politicians looking for favors. There's plenty of committee work as well, shepherding various bills and amendments through committee in hopes they'll reach the floor for an up down vote. In the midst of all this activity, it's vital I find out who the mole in our office is. I need something, an issue, an embarrassing secret, something to smoke him (or her) out. Meanwhile, life with Chloe is getting more interesting. This coming Friday will be our second date. I'm constantly thinking about her. She's the one positive in my life, an island of happiness in a sea of confusion.

We meet at a quiet restaurant in Crystal City and find ourselves sharing personal histories. Both her parents are accomplished in their respective fields; her mother, a world-class pianist; and her father, a labor lawyer. They insisted that she and her younger brother attend the best schools and set lofty goals for their lives. Her brother's a respected thoracic surgeon and she an accomplished attorney. They're well on their way to achieving the goals set out for them by their parents. We talk about our earliest childhood memories, summer vacations, and quirky relatives. She's the child of a nuclear family and knows little of her relatives. As is often the case when two people are attracted to each other, they bring complementary experiences. My family is big, extended, and raucous. Family gatherings are about who can talk the loudest and drown out the other with convincing, if totally biased, arguments. My parents have been active participants, and all of the cousins often stayed at one another's houses, especially over the summer. It's what feeds my love for politics. After all, Congress is one big, noisy, totally biased family that argues over anything and everything.

As the evening flows, we come to realize that our relationship has moved from a couple of dates to a desire to spend more time together. Admittedly, when we first met at Liddy's, it was Chloe's beauty that caught my attention. But now her unassuming demeanor, openness, and lack of agenda have nourished my interest. Finally and sadly, it's time to leave. We say good night with a kiss that lasts long enough for both of us to know this is real. While still in each other's arms Chloe quietly says, "Mark, I hope we can continue to see each other."

Flooded with the reality that we are falling for each other, I press my lips to hers and then bring them close to her ear and whisper, "So do I."

A beep from the grinning taxi driver finally separates us. As the cab pulls away, she says, "Call me in the morning."

I decide to take the long walk from Dupont Circle down to the Mall and back to my apartment. For a few hours, I'm able to put aside the anxiety of the past couple of weeks and enjoy the lingering warmth of Chloe's presence.

I'm pausing in front of the reflecting pool with the Capitol as a backdrop when my cell phone vibrates. It's after 11:00 p.m. and the number is not familiar. Who could be calling?

"Is this Mark Burnham?" says a voice I don't recognize.

"Yes, what can I do for you?"

"You don't know me but we have a mutual friend in Professor Wilson."

OK, this guy really has my attention—especially since he refers to Chuck in the present tense.

"The professor mailed me a copy of a very interesting research paper by a Mr. Theodore Edelstein. He asked me to review it and get back to him and you with what I found out."

"You never mentioned your name."

"Oh, sorry, I'm Steven Freeman. The professor engages me from time to time. I'm a researcher by training and profession. He sent the paper over with a request to examine the author's various conclusions as well as to look into 'The Carbon Conspiracy.' Unfortunately, I've been in Europe for the past month doing some research for the New York

Public Library on the history of medieval gargoyles. I only arrived home late this afternoon and found the package from Chuck."

That answers my second question. "You haven't heard about Chuck, then?"

With caution in his voice he replies, "No."

"He died under suspicious circumstances a week ago."

"What! That can't be."

I assure him it's true.

He wants to know what I mean by suspicious. I walk him through the events as I know them, along with the initial rendering by police that it was a suicide.

"That's not possible," he assures me. "The professor was not that kind of person."

"His niece and I already came to that conclusion and she's engaged an independent medical examiner to conduct a second autopsy."

All this leaves Freeman at a loss. He rambles for a few minutes about what a great colleague Chuck was and the terrible loss, personal and professional, his death means to him. He's about to hang up when I remind him that he called me for a reason.

"Steve, did anything Chuck send you catch your attention?" I know he'd just opened the package a few hours ago. I expect a negative response and hope he'll engage in some quick research.

"Oh yes, I'm very familiar with the Carbon Conspiracy. The points made in Edelstein's paper support what I know."

I've been hijacked several times by people dropping the conspiracy bomb and grow suspicious. "And just how could you learn so much in just a few hours?"

"I couldn't. Chuck was aware that I'd engaged in a study several years back that drew on publicly available information to hypothesize the existence of a giant conspiracy."

With that, I remember Chuck's last words about checking with someone. Steve must be the one.

It's going on midnight when I encourage him to continue, as I stand alone on the Mall with a few of Washington's homeless asleep nearby.

"The Economic Council for Integrity in Business hired me to conduct what was supposed to be a relatively mundane study of the various factors that move the financial markets. In particular, they were interested in how world events affect the supply of oil, which in turn drives financial markets up or down, depending on the news. During my research, I came across an article from the *Times* that said the New York attorney general's office had indicted a group of young investors, many of whom were related, for engaging in insider trading. According to the charges, they used insider information to pit trading in oil and other commodities on the New York and London Commodities markets against stocks of certain blue-chip companies on the Dow. The attorney general's office suggested that executives inside these companies were leaking information."

Connie Imlen had leveled a similar charge in her paper.

"Were any companies in particular mentioned?" I ask with some trepidation.

He thinks for a moment. "I recall a couple of the big oil companies, which was no surprise, and one old-line conglomerate, Con-Gen Industries."

Could Con-Gen and the WW9 have been involved?

"Who was the family to whom the article referred?"

"Somehow that information was withheld."

"What ever happened to the indictment?"

"It was quietly dismissed. When the *Times* called the attorney general's office to inquire, they were told, 'No comment.'"

"Were you able to find out anything further?"

"Funny you should ask. Given whom you work for, I assumed you might know."

My curiosity kicks into high gear. "What do you mean?"

"I contacted a friend who worked in the attorney general's office at the time to find out what he knew. The guy was a bit circumspect, but what I gathered is that the attorney general received a call from Congressman Trendle's office suggesting he drop the investigation."

As an afterthought, I ask, "Steve, I've been trying to track down how someone who used to be a high-profile scientist with the Nuclear Regulatory Agency might be connected with all this."

He immediately responds, "You wouldn't happen to be referring to Professor Imlen, would you?"

"As a matter of fact, yes," I reply with surprise.

"The professor was working for TCC at the time as its in-house environmental consultant. It was she who alerted me to Con-Gen's role in the scandal."

"Why didn't her name ever surface in connection with this?" I ask.

"Connie's husband was seriously ill and she couldn't afford to lose her job. She contacted me to provide background, but would not allow her name to be used."

Somehow, Connie survived as long as she did because of the information she held over their heads. It was also evident that her submission of the paper was the final act that forced TCC's hand.

Thanking him for the information, I promise to keep in touch. My head is spinning as I walk to my apartment. How could I have worked in Trendle's office these past seven years, risen to chief of staff, and not know about this? Trendle confides everything in me, or so I thought. At the time it occurred, I would not have been on anyone's radar. This has to be something so sensitive that Trendle felt he could trust nobody. I need to track it down.

Over the weekend, I spend several hours documenting what I know about every member of Trendle's office staff. One of them has to be keeping tabs on me. Having ruled out Trendle, since his schedule makes it virtually impossible for him to keep tabs on anyone, I focus on Shauna next. She's the longest-serving member of his team and probably knows more about the skeletons in his closet than anyone else knows. I eventually rule her out for two reasons. She's too obvious a candidate and thus unlikely the one to whom the WW9 would turn. Further, after listening to her fiancé, Albert's, impassioned plea for seeking the truth behind global warming, it occurs to me that Shauna's too pure, too innocent to engage in anything subversive. However, I make a note to talk to her about what Steven Freeman, Chuck Wilson's researcher, shared with me. If anyone knows about Trendle's intervention with the New York attorney general, she would. I make notes on each of the remaining staffers, listing the pros and cons of them being the snitch. In the end, I eliminate all but Kevin Riggs. I'd almost forgotten about him, as he's an intern in the office and generally only shows up a couple of days each week. After weighing the evidence, I have a growing suspicion that he's the one. Riggs is a graduate student majoring in an obscure field of international economics at Downstate University. When not in the office he is presumably deeply immersed in writing his thesis.

But something about Kevin doesn't add up. In a break from the normal vetting process, Kevin was introduced to me on the Monday that he started. I had no opportunity to interview him, which was standard procedure with prospective interns. He was not only a graduate student but older than most interns, which is unusual. The principle point of suspicion, however, is that he never shows any enthusiasm regarding his area of expertise. Yes, Kevin can answer questions about international economics satisfactorily, but he never expresses the typical know-it-all intern enthusiasm about changing the world.

First thing Monday, I call Downstate's School of Graduate Studies and pitch them a story that we had a congressional complaint about Kevin's financial aid. This isn't all that unusual, as our office frequently contacts the various universities within the state about constituents' complaints that financial aid was denied to their sons or daughters.

The office puts me on hold for a few minutes, after which a woman comes on the line and with some confusion states, "Mr. Burnham, there must be some mistake. Kevin Riggs does not receive financial aid. His tuition was paid in full at the beginning of the semester."

I'm about to thank her and hang up when, as an afterthought, I ask, "Has Kevin paid his tuition at the beginning of every semester?" I hear some tapping on a keyboard then she's back on the line.

"This is Kevin's first semester at the university. He transferred in from another graduate program." After confirming that the records did not specify which program, I thank her and hang up, wondering if university records were altered to provide an educational cover story for Riggs.

It takes me several days to conjure up a scheme that would uncover his duplicity. I stop by his desk when he shows up Wednesday. "Hey, Kevin, stop by my office. I have a project for you that's right up your alley."

A few minutes later, he dutifully comes in, notebook in hand, conveying a look of expectancy. I brief him on some routine piece of legislation. "Listen, we have an opportunity to influence the development of Third World wind-to-power projects. Trendle wants to include some support material that demonstrates the projects make sense economically. Can you dig up relevant literature and pull together a summary paragraph that lends academic support?"

I know Kevin is a Redskins fan, as the wallpaper on this computer screen features the team's logo. I drop the red herring, seemingly as an afterthought. "Did you see the article the other day on the outrageous club and luxury boxes at FedEx Field?"

He laughs. "Sure goes to show you how much power and money football generates."

"What I wouldn't give for access. Great way to see a game," I say in a joking manner. After a pause, I continue, "Fat chance. We are but lowly staffers."

Kevin nods in agreement. We quickly get back to discussing the research project and finish a few minutes later. "I'm on it," he remarks, leaving the office.

Actually, I prefer to watch football on TV but visitors sometimes use high-priced tickets to try and buy some influence. Usually, we graciously refuse them, as it is not only unethical but also illegal to accept such gifts. However, I've known more than a few staffers who quietly take such gifts, knowing that the odds are against them being caught.

Sitting back in my chair, I wonder if Kevin will take the bait. Fortunately, there's little time to dwell on this question, as we're deeply immersed in trying to rescue the Pittfield hearing. Trendle's making a great show of it. He's seen everywhere talking with reporters, meeting with the governor of Florida, and huddled with environmental watchdog groups.

He has me appear on CNN's *Politics Today*, one of the more liberal and environmentally friendly televised roundtable forums. Two scientists and I engage in a virtual group hug while simultaneously bashing Big Oil, predicting the demise of the Earth as we know it and mourning the imminent extinction of several species of fish. After thirty minutes of this, the host brings it to a close. I'm satisfied that we made a good showing even though I know it was a smoke-and-mirrors performance. There's an unwritten rule of thumb that important legislation and political victories are achieved quietly; otherwise, nine times out of ten the opportunity is lost.

Quite frankly, what we're engaged in is political damage control to cover our own fumbling of this opportunity and the behind-the-scenes deal-making that led Trendle to abandon the attack. The icing on the cake is something we have no control over, but ensures that Pittfield will not suffer. The weather betrays us as prevailing winds and currents shift just enough that the slick moves away from the Keys, giving Pittfield time to clean it up. This, in turn, means the press completely loses interest. The shear energy used in putting on this face-saving show actually renews my sense of optimism and I began to look forward to the next political battle.

And then there's Saturday with Chloe. It is amazing how the promise of a continuing relationship with a wonderful woman can make one bounce back from a black mood.

Before leaving the office on Friday, I call Shauna into my office. "I'm looking for files regarding that conspiracy thing from the New York attorney general's office Trendle was dealing with." Better to play dumb so as not to alert her that this was anything other than routine.

Without hesitation, she replies, "I don't recall, but if you have the dates I can check the congressman's schedule." I give her the dates, which she takes back to her desk. I hear the clicking of her keyboard and then she returns a few minutes later.

"I found an appointment for a teleconference with the attorney general a few days after the date you gave me." I ask if she remembers the nature of the meeting. "No, that was several years back and there are no notes on file connected with the meeting."

"Does it say who arranged the meeting?"

After a pause' "Yes your predecessor."

That explains Melanie's sudden disappearance.

This officially eliminates Shauna: she was not the least bit concerned with my inquiry. It also tells me that Trendle must have handled the meeting personally, because Shauna normally keeps a record of every meeting she coordinates.

TWENTY-TWO

Chloe and I decide to see a play at the Kennedy Center and have a late dinner in Georgetown. Chloe's staying at the law firm's apartment in Crystal City, a few blocks from the Pentagon. She's now on extended assignment in DC, working on a legal matter with the Department of Justice. I knock on her door shortly before 7:00 p.m. After a few moments, it opens. She's wearing a bright print dress that matched my mood and the look on her face tells me she's as eager to see me as I am to see her. She grabs her purse and we catch a cab to the Kennedy Center.

Crossing the Key Bridge, she moves closer and I wrap my arm around her as we kiss. We could ride around all evening just holding each other. What more could I ask for? Chloe's beautiful, intelligent, and enjoys sharing her passions, desires, and beliefs with me as much as I do with her.

During the performance, we held hands and spend more time looking at each other than at the stage. After the performance, we decide to take a leisurely walk out of DC proper into Georgetown, enjoying the beautiful spring evening and each other's company. No words need to be spoken. If this is the definition of perfection, then sign me up. With Chloe, my life's about to change in ways I can scarcely imagine.

I spot a restaurant on Wisconsin Avenue and ask the hostess for a quiet spot. With a knowing smile, she directs us to a cozy table that's equally suited to spies exchanging secrets as it is to lovers exchanging hearts. The wine is smooth and the steaks are perfect. Finishing our dinner, we quietly talk of what little we can remember of the performance. Bonds of affection have stolen our attention from the illusion on stage.

Chloe takes my hand as I look deeply into her smiling, hazel eyes. "Mark, I have something for you."

I start to protest, as I have nothing to give her in return. She puts her finger to my lips. "I think you know I have developed deep feelings for you."

Nodding, I reveal the same to her.

"My extended stay in DC is no accident. I managed to convince the firm to assign the legal work with Justice to me so I could spend more time with you." Reaching into her purse, she extracts a slim, gift-wrapped box and slides it across the table.

"Happy birthday!"

With a mixture of surprise and mirth, I reply, "But my birthday isn't for three months.

"I know," she replies coyly. "But I wanted to let you know how much I care for you." Again, I start to protest feeling bad that I don't have anything for her. "That's why it's a birthday gift. Go ahead and open it."

With much anticipation, I slip the gold paper off and open the box. A chill goes through my body and I can feel the sweat beginning to form on my forehead. I stare at what's inside, completely at a loss for words. After a minute, she asks if something's wrong. To cover the shock, fear, and hint of betrayal that's beginning to enter my consciousness, I shoot back, "No, no, this is perfect. I was caught by surprise as the season is four months away and the cost...you shouldn't have spent so much."

Relief spreads across her face as she incorrectly assumes the shock is related to the expense of the tickets.

"I know how much you love the Redskins."

I'm hoping she spent her own money in spite of the small print at the bottom of the tickets that reads: Courtesy of Becht, Chalmers & Davidson.

"Besides, they didn't cost me a dime. The firm always has tickets to the box and club level well in advance of the fall season and I pleaded that I wanted to give my new boyfriend something special."

What can I say? My emotions are in turmoil, my intestines tied up in knots. It seems impossible that Chloe is out to get me. Our feelings are all too real, or so it seems. Yet it's inconceivable that this is a happy coincidence. Less than a week after I baited the hook and dangled it under Kevin's nose, Chloe's giving me these tickets.

My thoughts are on overdrive as my heart sinks. Why her? She's the last person I would have wanted it to be. Is she an innocent pawn for the firm, or is this a sinister act on Chloe's part? The evening is a bust, and yet I'm not prepared to give up on her. To cover my discomfort and put some space between us, I confess that I'm not feeling well, that it may have been the oysters I had as an appetizer. Her look of concern seems genuine. While I pay the bill, she hails a cab and drops me at my apartment.

"Promise me you will call me first thing in the morning."

"I will," I say, weakly.

Walking straight from the front door to the fridge, I grab a beer, pop the cap, and suck long and hard from the bottle. Staring at the tickets, two questions loom large: What does this mean, and more importantly, who exactly is behind it? I'm desperate to believe Chloe's the innocent pawn, yet she's an experienced attorney. She has to know these tickets put my career and possibly my freedom in jeopardy. Long gone are the days when lobbyists can slip casual gifts to influential staffers. Violations of the Gift Act come with criminal penalties. Still, it is possible that the boys at Becht, especially her oily boss, Harry, managed to convince her that since no money changed hands it's OK. I can come to no conclusion about Chloe's involvement and the uncertainty assures a sleepless night.

The rest of the weekend is depressing as I realize how alone I am. Chloe had become my lifeline during this difficult time dealing with the recent deaths and tongue-lashings from the WW9 crew. The possibility of her betrayal plunges me even deeper into despair. Thinking back over the times we spent together, I'm grateful for one thing. I never told her the real reason I contacted Chuck. It does occur to me that Chloe seemed especially interested in the circumstances surrounding his death. That in itself is not incriminating. After all, her concern and desire to comfort me made it perfectly natural that she would want me to talk it through. Yet I have to consider the possibility of another hidden agenda.

Ever since high school, I've always maintained control no matter what the circumstances or threats. The defining moment was junior year. A major cheating scandal erupted that threatened my chances of finishing the year with honors. Since the culprit had not come forward, the entire class's standing was at risk. Like most high school cheating schemes, the students knew who was behind it long before the teachers did. With my future at risk, I cornered the senior who was selling the exams and browbeat him into confessing in front of the principal.

I came away with two valuable lessons from this experience. First, I realized I had the gift of constructive arguing and, once convinced I was right, could best most opponents in a verbal duel. The second lesson was that retribution is just around the corner. Two days later, several of the recipients of the stolen answers cornered me in the locker room and threatened to kick my ass. Thinking fast, I told them I was taking over the exam scam and could supply answers at half what they were paying my predecessor. It was Machiavellian to be sure, but survival demanded a devious response. These morons—two football stars and a pothead—were too stupid and greedy to ask how I magically had gained access to the exam masters. The breathing room this deal provided allowed me to feed them the answers to the calculus final. Not surprisingly, they each managed to flunk the exam with grades approaching zero. A day later, they were called before the principal and asked why they each had exactly the same wrong answers. After much shuffling of feet and looking at the floor, one of them admitted he had cheated and then quickly tried to blame me. Needless to say, the principal did not believe him. But he did call me in to confront me with the accusation. I looked the principal straight in the eye and emphatically stated, "Why would I give them the wrong answers? What kind of cheating scam is that, anyway?" The principal caught the fleeting expression of triumph that crossed my face. I always suspected he knew that I had engineered the whole thing but decided that justice had prevailed.

My approach to all subsequent challenges has been the same: vanquish the enemy and take no prisoners. It's allowed me to surge ahead of the pack. This present crisis, however, is like nothing I've ever experienced. It runs deeper, has deadly consequences, and grows more sinister as events unfold. It's not something I can handle alone. I need an ally, someone I can trust without question.

First I need to put some space between Chloe without arousing suspicion. As deeply hurt as I am by Chloe's deception, intended or not, she could prove to be a point of entry to solving the mystery. As much as I hate to do it, I decide to pretend all is well. I call her that afternoon to let her know that I'm feeling better and that I need to break our date this coming Friday because of a key legislative deadline. I did ask if she would like to go away with me the following weekend. Intrigued, she responds in her silkiest voice, "What did you have in mind?"

"Now, you wouldn't want me to spoil the surprise. After all, maybe it's your birthday. We should celebrate."

The lightness in her voice tells me she bought it. If in fact Chloe's an innocent player in some larger drama, I don't want to lose her, and I would indeed take her on a weekend getaway. The two weeks gives me a bit of breathing room to engineer some misdirection. When an organization is threatened, especially if it is something scandalous, it invariably engages in a campaign of disinformation, which, if pursued, can become its undoing.

I decide to push Senator Plesher's buttons and see what emerges.

Libertarians for Freedom from Corporate Influence is a small 503c Political Action Committee whose principal mission is to eliminate the power and influence that large corporations hold over the political process. This PAC is peculiar in that it's comprised of aggressive lobbyists who devote much of their energy to complaining about lobbyists. What gives them muscle is the heavy financial and influential backing they receive from Ted Tuckerman, a billionaire who's determined to use his money to atone for the sins he committed to accumulate it. Of course, the idea of donating the vast bulk of his wealth to a worthy charity never seems to occur to him.

LFCI is not a random choice. I knew from surfing the web that Tuckerman loathes the good Senator Plesher because of her cozy relationship with corporate America. If I can get a bit of juicy gossip in front of him, with enough evidence to make it convincing, he will blog, tweet, Facebook, and otherwise steamroll Plesher and Con-Gen into some kind of response. Then it's a matter of keeping the pressure on until they slip up, revealing whatever darker truth exists.

I need to feed the information to him without leaving evidence of my involvement. It's less about fear and more about the realization that if I'm seen as part of this too early in the game, they'll simply take me down. After two days of online research, I find my scandal. Con-Gen had constructed an oil pipeline in southeastern Montana to move the expanded flow of oil from recently revitalized oil fields. A section of pipe that crossed Jake Lacey's farm sprang a leak and flooded eight acres with thousands of gallons of crude oil. Con-Gen repaired the leak, cleaned up the field, and paid Jake an undisclosed sum with the written understanding that he would keep his mouth shut. Unfortunately for Con-Gen, farmer Jake was more than happy to take the money, sign the nondisclosure, and then completely ignore the agreement by bashing Con-Gen at every opportunity. What made this scandal ideal is that the farm is in Plesher's hometown and yet she came to the solid defense of Con-Gen. The local press picked up the squabble and published an expose titled, "Plesher and Con-Gen Together Again." For a small-town paper, it had a gusty editor willing to piss off an influential senator and a powerful company, leaving local politicians fearful that federal subsidy money would suddenly dry up.

I took a chance, printed the articles, and faxed them over to Mabis asking her what she knows. E-mails are too easy to monitor. Three days later, a printout mysteriously appears in my in-basket. It's a chain of e-mails between Plesher and Con-Gen, discussing Jake Lacey's lack of cooperation. Their arrogance, the coziness of their relationship, and their utter disdain for the farmer leaps off the pages. At one point, they refer to him as "the stupid farmer that needs to be eliminated." The beauty of an e-mail printout is that it has all the addresses, dates, and times needed to verify the correspondence is genuine, but it has no electronic link to Mabis. I have no idea how she got hold of them.

TWENTY-THREE

To minimize suspicion I decide to reach out to someone other than Josh. "Hey, Don, how goes it?" I ask while sliding onto the bar stool next to him. Don is one of those seasoned, if somewhat cynical beat reporters who feeds news to the Hill rags that report the day-to-day activity in Congress. Most of it too insider and mundane to be of much interest to the American public. There are, of course, exceptions, which guys like Don live for. I've used Don in the past to leak information that Trendle wanted to test the American public with while remaining anonymous. That way, he either could be for or against it, depending on which way the polls indicated voters felt about the issue.

Throwing me that world-weary look, he mouths, "OK, Mark, what do you want this time?"

"Hey, you're way too suspicious."

"That's what a good reporter's supposed to be," he says, as he turns his attention to the bucket of bar snacks.

"Not to worry. Just wanted to buy you a beer. After all I owe you one for that exposé on Big Oil's assault on the Alaska National Preserve."

"Thanks. So how come it took so long to buy me that beer?"

"Time flies when one is slaving away for Trendle. He has me running six ways at once, pushing wind power uphill against a ton of political hot air."

"I'll bet. Why don't you and the congressman give up on wind, anyway? The nuclear advocates would love to have Trendle as their champion."

I grimace. "Fat chance. Besides, all our green friends would turn on us."

"I suppose supporting anything practical is beneath the WW9," he sarcastically shoots back. The fact that he knows that "WW9" is the nickname Trendle and I use momentarily catches me off guard. But I figure reporters pick up all kinds of info as they pound their beats.

"True enough," I concede. "Can I buy you a second beer?"

"A two-beer favor? You must really be desperate."

"Nothing could be further from the truth," I say, yawning with as much indifference as I can muster. "In fact, what I have in my pocket is a career builder for you."

He leans his dumpy frame back on the stool and looks down his nose at me through the horn-rimmed glasses he perpetually wears. He's clearly suspicious. Any reporter as experienced as Don knows there's no quid without the pro quo.

I hand over the clippings from the Montana newspaper first. Better to whet his appetite and reel him in slowly. Don scans the articles, turns to me, and says, "Interesting. I agree it could have been sensational, but regurgitating something that has already made the local press will do nothing for my career. Looks like you wasted good beer, but thanks anyway." As he gets up to leave, he sees the sly grin on my face and sits back down. "There's more, isn't there?"

The smirk morphs into a smile. Still I say nothing. I want him to make the next move. Finally, he lets out a long breath and reaches out. "OK, hand it over."

I pull the e-mail printouts between Plesher and Con-Gen out of my jacket pocket and slide it across to him. He begins to read the e-mails as I stand up to leave. If he finds something interesting, and I'm sure he will, an article will appear quoting an unnamed source. No evidence of my involvement will ever emerge.

As I turn to leave, I add, "Don, I really think you should share this info with your friend at LCFI."

It was his turn to be surprised. "How do you know?"

"We all have our little secrets." It's the reason I picked Don. He and Tuckerman are known to coordinate their public attacks on Plesher.

Two days later, the first of what turns out to be a series of articles hits the press. It focuses on the long-standing and cozy relationship between Con-Gen and the senator. Don links Con-Gen's extensive fund-raising on Plesher's behalf to her willingness to assure that the Energy Committee, which she chairs, approves deep oil-drilling permits.

T.C. Clarkson's name is mentioned as well. He'll be furious. I can only imagine the heated conversations he's having with WW9 and Plesher. It's sure to be ugly. Don also hints that Plesher and Con-Gen had ganged up on Jake Lacey, the struggling farmer in Montana. That fact that Jake's a wealthy rancher, receives enormous agricultural subsidies, and Con-Gen continues to pay him to let them move oil across his land is irrelevant. By portraying him as the little guy powerless to stop big business and big politics, Don gets his readers' attention, and more quickly than I imagined, the *Times* wants to collaborate with him on a national story.

Don does a masterful job suggesting that Con-Gen was not above bundling donations to fatten Plesher's campaign war chest illegally. Bundling involves a person or organization collecting money from a syndicate of donors and presenting a single, very large check. Con-Gen was, of course, too clever to be that obvious. Don, in turn, is too shrewd to accuse Con-Gen openly. Instead, he lets the record speak for itself. In reviewing the public fund-raising and lobbying records, Don noticed a pattern of the same four or five corporate and individual donors attending every fund-raising event Con-Gen hosted for Plesher. By listing them by name, he implies bundling without explicitly stating it. Despite having been the source, I'm shocked to see the names Jane Preston, the youngest of the Rumple Sisters, and Malcolm Little on the list. What did the WW9 care about oil fields in Montana?

Best of all, Don shares what he knows with LCFI. The timing is beautiful. With the papers and network news buzzing about the Plesher scandal, and the thousands of bloggers who hang on every blip from LCFI, Plesher and Con-Gen's phones are ringing off the hook.

They'll undoubtedly survive this mini scandal. The challenge is to add fuel to the fire while it's still hot. Now I'm sure that the reference to "CS" that Professor Chuck Wilson tucked into his Bible mean "carbon scandal." Chuck was looking into this as well; the call I received from Steven Freeman confirmed that. The problem is I have no real evidence. The reference might have been enough for Don to run with, but since I took the evidence from Chuck's office, it's tainted. Thinking about Teddy's background at the EPA I have an idea.

The next morning, I phone a friend whom I got to know early in my career. At the time, she was a staffer on the House Energy Committee, but she quickly decided she'd rather be working on the agency side, away from congressional politics. She landed at the General Accounting Office (GAO), which has a host of obscure but vitally important functions meant to insure our government does what it's supposed to do with honesty and integrity. If the GAO were simply engaged in analysis, producing endless reports for Congress and the public, it would quickly become as irrelevant as the thousands of blue-ribbon panels created to pontificate about every aspect of government action or inaction. In fact, the GAO wields enormous influence because it's empowered to investigate allegations of illegal and improper activities and issue legal decisions and opinions, such as bid protest rulings and reports on agency rules. As the congressional watchdog, this supposedly nonpartisan agency can make life hell for those it is investigating. Likewise, the GAO is often the pathway to tax-supported profits with those corporations they choose to ignore. Billions of dollars hang in the balance every time GAO renders a bid-protest decision. And when the dollars are that large, the loser protests virtually every bid decision.

"I'm unavailable to take your call at this time. Please leave a message."

"Kelly, its Mark Burnham. I need to run something by you when you have a minute."

Agency officials seldom answer their phones directly. Voice mail gives them a chance to screen callers. Sure enough, ten minutes later my phone rings.

"Mark, it's great to hear from you!"

Kelly and I quickly became Hill buddies and we continue to maintain contact when either of us needs information. "So, how's the exciting world of GAO?"

"Who could ask for more? We're the agency that manages nothing but gets to stick our bureaucratic noses into the business of every other department," she says with a laugh.

"That's why I love you."

"How come you only love me when you need something?" she shoots back, engaging in the mandatory trash talk before we get down to business.

With the preliminaries out of the way, I quickly get to the point. "I'm trying to track down any government reports authored by a Theodore Edelstein during his time with the

EPA." I provide dates for his tenure at the agency as well as his subsequent billet with the Oil Association.

"Wow, your guy really did cross a line in the sand with that career move," she notes. "What in particular are you looking for?"

I explain the obscure reference to a conspiracy.

"I'll take a look and if I find anything I'll call you back first thing in the morning." There's a pause on the phone before she says, "It seems to me it would be a whole lot simpler to ask him directly."

"I would, but he was killed in an accident several weeks ago."

"I guess that won't work, then. Let me see what I can find out." With that, she hangs up.

The rest of the morning is taken up with routine business with representatives of various nonprofit environmental groups, a few phone calls from influential local politicos looking for favors, and reworking Trendle's fund-raising schedule for the nth time.

Halfway through a sandwich in the House cafeteria the following day, my cell rings. "Boy, do I have something for you," Kelly says excitedly. "That Edelstein guy authored one explosive white paper."

I grab a couple of napkins and begin to take notes. "When was it published?"

I can hear Kelly tapping on the keyboard. "Looks like we logged it three months before he left EPA."

Once the leadership at EPA caught wind of this paper, there would have been enormous pressure for him to leave.

"It seems the main premise of the paper was that the Environmental Protection Agency is rife with organizational conflict of interest (OCI) that resulted in lopsided and grossly unfair application of regulations," she says.

"Kelly, I need specifics."

"OK, here goes." With that she starts to read off the paper while I scribble as fast as I can, trying to keep up.

"After a brief introduction, he starts listing pieces of evidence supporting his assertion," she continues.

"For the third time in the past eighteen months Con-Gen was cited by EPA for gross negligence," Kelly reads. "Two times for faulty high-voltage transmission-line infractions and once for an improperly installed oil pipeline. Each time, a scheduled inspection was cancelled at the last minute due to the influence of Senator Plesher."

I interrupt. "How did Teddy know this?"

"Be patient, I'm getting to that," Kelly testily fires back. "Edelstein reports that on two of the inspections, he was the scientist in charge and was told directly by the director that Plesher called to insist they back down. He reports that a colleague who was in charge of the third inspection told him that he received a similar message from the director."

I can easily imagine that all Plesher had to do was imply funding cuts and the director, a political appointee hoping for future advancement, was all too ready to acquiesce.

"He then goes on to say how the EPA deliberately ignores the slaughter of tens of thousands of birds by windmills yet vilifies the oil companies every time a seagull gets drenched in oil," Kelly continues.

OK, I can see Teddy's point, but this did not make for the kind of scandal that would bring down an empire.

With disappointment evident in my voice I say, "Kelly, these are serious allegations, but I'm hoping for something more. If this is all there is, then I'll have to look elsewhere."

"Whoa there, cowboy. Who said anything about being finished? I've saved the best for last." She then reveals the eight-hundred-pound gorilla in the white paper. "Edelstein charges that senior officials at EPA, Con-Gen, Plesher, and an unnamed group of influential investors were manipulating the securities markets in a complex scheme of insider trading that pits stocks against options and commodity futures."

The "influential investors" must be the WW9. This jells with what Freeman told me about the "family members" involved in insider trading.

She goes on. "Edelstein also suggests that this scheme extends to a member of the Supreme Court."

"Did he mention who the justice was?" I ask, surprised and saddened at the same time.

After a few moments, she comes back. "No, all the report says is that due to his influence, several close votes came out in support of the scheme."

It has to be Kensington. And if he was the one, then Chloe had to be involved as well. The criminal act of a stranger is one thing. The betrayal by someone I'm falling for is tearing my heart to shreds.

"Mark, are you still on the line?"

"Yes, sorry. Thanks, Kelly. I owe you one."

With Kelly still on the line, I let out a long slow breath, thinking we just hit the mother of all scandals. Birds, one can overlook. Missed inspections can be explained. But securities fraud can bring down corporate empires no matter how big and well insulated they are. "Does Teddy provide any evidence supporting this allegation?" I ask.

"He mentions he is researching this and intends to submit a subsequent paper. He does say that the securities involve oil, lithium, and certain stocks that make up the Dow."

I ask Kelly if she can fax the report over to me and to my surprise, she declines.

"Mark, you know I'd do anything for you, but GAO is sensitive to leaks of whistle-blower info, which this is considered. I'd be fired in a minute if I did."

I certainly don't want to get her in trouble. "Understood. I have just one last question. Why didn't GAO go public with this?"

She sighs and says, "You wouldn't believe the amount of whistle-blower e-mails, letters, and white papers we receive from disgruntled employees. Most turn out to be bogus, but the law is such that the author is protected. In turn, we don't go public unless we can verify the accusation from other sources. Edelstein's report was in the pending file and could remain there for several years," she says.

I thank her and hang up.

What has just been revealed is explosive. But how can I take advantage of it? Some of the info is obvious. The Dow company tied in with Plesher and the Montana fields had to be Con-Gen. But I can't figure lithium into the equation. I need to engage someone who understands how Wall Street works, someone who's an insider. A name comes to mind. He's perfect except for one small problem. He is currently a guest at the minimum-security federal penitentiary in Birdsboro, West Virginia.

TWENTY-FOUR

I've been trying to convince myself that Chloe could have been an innocent pawn but her obvious involvement with Kensington changes all this. I need to find out to whom Kevin Riggs is feeding the information regarding my whereabouts and conversations. In all likelihood, Chloe is a recipient of the info, not Riggs's contact. I have to follow Riggs and really need the help of Chet Southers, the PI. My paranoia, justifiable in these circumstances, makes me leery of calling Southers on any of my phones. On the way back from the Capitol, after a series of interim floor votes related to some obscure legislation, I stop in to visit the office of South Dakota's lone congressman, Norm Sethman. I know his chief of staff, Dan Anderson well, as his boss and mine recently cosponsored a bill imposing a surcharge tax on land currently under lease where new and deeper oil wells are being sunk. There's no chance it will pass, but it offers Trendle yet another opportunity to make a point.

"Mark, what windmill blew you in here?" While Dan and his boss have worked with us on several fronts, they both think Trendle's obsession with windmills is nutty.

"All's well," I lie. "And no, I'm not here to talk about renewable energy, something you should take more of an interest in. Wonder if I could use your phone," I casually ask. "Too lazy to go back to my office and my cell needs a recharge."

Without a moment's hesitation, he points to the empty conference room, where I place a call to Southers's office. His receptionist must have heard the anxiety in my voice because this time he comes on the line right away.

"Mark, didn't expect to hear from you again so soon."

I give him the five-minute version of the latest happenings with an emphasis on Edelstein and Chuck's deaths, and the mole in our office.

"I need a few days to collect some background on this. I'll call you on Friday."

"There's a problem with that," I say. "I think my phones are bugged."

"If that's true, you're in deep water, my friend." He thinks for a moment. "I assume you are not calling me on your phone now."

I assure him I'm not.

"OK my standard retainer is two grand. We need to meet and I think you need a weekend away because you're still struggling with your friend's death." He outlines a plan to meet over the weekend. "This getaway will give you cover for the large sum of money you have to withdraw. If your phones are being tapped, then undoubtedly they're monitoring your bank accounts and credit cards." With that, he hangs up. I make a second quick call to New York and leave the office, thanking Dan on the way out.

I catch the 4:00 p.m. Amtrak to New York the nest day and meet Chuck's niece, Emily Snow, at Milligan's, an Irish pub near Penn Station. We hug and sit at a quiet table where we can talk without being overheard. Before I can open my mouth, she blurts out: "Mark, you were right. The autopsy results from the private medical examiner came back showing dangerous levels of carbon monoxide in his system."

"Did he say how it got there?"

"Apparently, the only way is the common one. He breathed it in over a period of time."

"I'm surprised the cops didn't try and convince you that it could still be suicide," I say. "Carbon monoxide is a common method for taking one's life."

"The forensic doctor I hired pointed out the lack of a source of the gas and other medical factors, and convinced the police that it couldn't have been suicide after all," she responds.

"How come the city medical examiner missed it?"

"The detective mumbled something to the effect that they don't normally look for it in a routine suicide," she says. "The good news is they're reopening the investigation."

As Emily talks, a battle between two opposing emotions begins to take place within me. On one hand, I still remember the cheerful teenage girl whose mom, Chuck's sister, would sometimes bring her to the campus to visit Uncle Professor Charley, as they always called him. Judging by the woman before me, Chuck did a great job helping his sister bring her up. Emily's no longer a teenage girl, but a young, profoundly attractive woman, whose beauty emerges as I come to know and experience her pain and hurt and goodness. Still reeling from Chloe's betrayal, I'm not prepared for these feelings. I push them back into that little corner inside where one hides emotions too difficult to deal with. I can't betray the honor and loyalty I owe Chuck and I feel guilty for even entertaining the possibility of a relationship with Emily.

The look on my face must have scared her. "What's wrong," she asks, panic in her voice. "I thought you would be happy that we know he didn't take his own life."

"I am. But in some ways, this darkens the picture." I go on to explain what's transpired since we last met. Emily is genuinely concerned when I mention Chloe's role in the ticket setup.

"I need to get back to DC first thing in the morning. Can you do three things for me?"

With a newfound determination, she nods. "Anything, just name it."

"Keep the pressure on the police to ensure the investigation stays open. Once they close a case, it's almost impossible to reopen it. Then contact the *New York Post* and offer them an exclusive about your uncle's suicide-turned murder."

With a confused look on her face, she says, "I don't understand. If the police keep investigating, isn't that enough?"

"Emily, this smells of a major conspiracy that could have national implications." My political instinct developed over last seven years on the Hill kicks in. "We need to flush out whoever is behind this. And for that, we need the press."

After I explain what to say, she raises an eyebrow and gives me a flinty look that almost breaks into a smile. It's good to see this after the pain she's endured. It seems the hopeful heart cannot remain forever shrouded in gloom—though I suspect we won't see the light for some time yet.

I picked the *Post* because of its reputation for hounding city officials if it smells a cover-up. The paper had already carried a front-page headline, "Prof's Post. Butchered by Manhattan M.E." The reporter responsible for that article is someone to whom I've leaked info in the past on behalf of Trendle.

"Contact him and use my name as a reference." I'm about to leave when she stops me.

"You mentioned three things. What's the third?"

"Someone I'm fond of is mixed up in this and I need you to do some legal research involving a judge I believe she has considerable influence with."

"Who's the judge?"

"Associate Justice Kensington."

She let out a low whistle. "You're kidding. What am I looking for?"

"I'm not sure. Focus on decisions over the last four years in which he had the pivotal vote. In particular, cases that impact the profits of the oil industry or Con-Gen Industries."

"And your friend's name wouldn't happen to be Chloe?"

I hesitate, and then nod.

Thankfully, she doesn't press further. Discussing Chloe with Emily reminds me of something. I'm now thinking that the initials "CS" that Chuck scribbled in his Bible could refer to Chloe Sullivan, and not "carbon scandal."

Thursday morning finds me back in DC. At intervals throughout the day, I pull the maximum available via several ATMs around the city. Between bank ATMs and credit card cash advances, I'm able to withdraw ten grand. It's more than enough to cover Souther's fee but I will need travel cash as well. I only hope Southers's scheme for getting him the money undetected works. Friday morning at the office, I make a lot of noise about heading up to Atlantic City for a weekend of gambling.

Hitting the road midday Saturday, I'm at the Tango Hotel and Casino by four that afternoon. The Tango is one of the smaller casinos situated at the north end of the boardwalk. I check in and unsuccessfully try to catch a couple hours of sleep. My nerves are beginning to fray as I'm about to cross over from legitimate inquiry to what may prove to be dangerous and possibly illegal snooping.

I shower and dress in what I hope looks like gambler gear: white T-shirt, black jacket, designer jeans, and leather slip-ons. I eat dinner alone in one of those dark steakhouses found in every casino. As 8:00 p.m. approaches, I wander along the rows of gaming tables, seemingly undecided about where to lose my money. Finally, I stop and squeeze in at a crowded, twenty-five-dollar-minimum craps table. After a miss by the current shooter, I place my chips in the rack and keep bets to a minimum. Twenty-five dollars on the pass line and twenty-five dollar come bets.

A few minutes later, I feel a bump accompanied by, "Excuse me, friend, can you make some room?" Sliding over I look up and see its Southers. He looks like the quintessential loser betting on horses at the track. The yellow pants, pink shirt, checked jacket, and white bucks ensure everyone else thinks so as well. As the banker changes his cash for chips, he gives Southers the look of one who's seen too many of his kind pretending to be big-time rollers. As agreed, we show no sign of recognition. He drops his five hundred dollars worth of chips in the rack next to mine and begins to lay down bets. He plays until the action and noise level heat up. Finally, when the shooter throws sevens, there's a collective groan, Chet scoops up his chips, and saunters off.

Looking down, I realize he'd made the switch. What's left of my eight grand is now gone and the remains of his five hundred dollars is in front of me. I play for another half hour until the rest of the chips are gone and then head over to the bar and order a drink.

"Hey stud, buy me a drink."

Next to me is a drop-dead-gorgeous blonde squeezed into an impossibly tight skirt with a hemline that almost meets the plunging V of her top. She looks borderline illegal but after all, this is a casino. I buy her a drink and we draw close and talk nonsense to each other. After two drinks, she takes my hand, whispers in my ear, and leads me to the elevator bank that takes us to the Club level. As we exit the elevator, there sits Chet on one of the small couches scattered throughout the lounge.

"Well, Southers, I got him here. You owe me one." Winking at both of us, she turns, and with the sexiest walk I've ever seen, proceeds back to the elevator, leaving us alone.

Once I've recovered from the show, I turn to Chet. "This is certainly a unique way to engineer a meeting." As it turns out, he does a lot of work for the casino, finding deadbeat gamblers who owe it. Thus, he has the run of the place.

"And why the elaborate scheme to get the money to you? I could've of simply handed it over."

With the sigh of someone having to explain to a child how the world really works, he answers, "No you couldn't. If your accounts are being monitored, the people doing it are pros and know to look for the unexplained disappearance of ten thousand dollars. They look for disruptions in a person's regular spending habits. So we had to give them a plausible explanation for the missing money. A crowded craps table is ideal because there's no tracking of individual expenditure by the players. You drop your cash on the table, receive chips, and play."

"What about the security guys watching on video monitors?"

"Generally they focus on the banker and thrower," Southers says. "Besides, they cut me a lot of slack, given all the money I recover for them."

Sliding his lanky frame deeper into the couch, he places the tips of his fingers together and nods. "Mark, go over everything from the beginning. Leave nothing out, even though you've told me most of it already. I want to be sure nothing is overlooked."

I walk him through the sequence of events, beginning with the paper submitted by Connie Imlen and Trendle's slip of the tongue. Then I move on to my conversation with Teddy and his subsequent "accidental death." After I relay the information that the GAO had regarding the carbon conspiracy, Chet interrupts.

"You don't realize the importance of what you just told me, do you?"

I admit that Teddy's role in all this is mystifying.

He answers his own question. "This provides the motives for Edelstein's death and Chuck's death, as well as for the attention the WW9 are showering upon you. I'm not surprised about the autopsy. If powerful people are behind this, a payoff to the medical examiner is not unheard of."

When I get to the part about Chloe, my voice is noticeably strained. Chet knows I'm emotionally conflicted. As a result, he makes me go over every aspect of our relationship and repeat it two more times until he's satisfied.

"Mark, you have to face the fact that Chloe is deeply involved in the conspiracy. You should expect the worst."

I knew this already, but hearing Chet say it aloud is like a knife in the gut. Realizing someone has betrayed you for money is one thing; when love is involved, it's devastating.

He's very interested in the interrogation I experienced at the WW9 dinner party. I mention my surprise when Betty Preston, the matriarch of the Rumple Sisters, hurled the accusation at me. He nods. "Hold that thought for a moment. Tell me what in particular T.C. Clarkson asked."

"He wanted to know about the meeting I had with Chuck Wilson, what we discussed, and especially why. Both he and Malcolm Little were incensed that I would talk with an obvious enemy of Trendle."

"Anything else?"

"I did overhear a comment that passed between Betty and Malcolm about how fortunate it was that Wilson just happened to be out of the way before he dug too deep."

Chet looks at me intently and I know it's going to be a long night. "I need you to tell me everything you know about the Rumple Sisters, Liddy, T.C., and Malcolm."

After sharing what I know, he asks: "Has Professor Longworth or his grad assistant Bernie gotten back in touch with you?"

"No"

"I'm not surprised; somebody from that group has warned Longworth off."

His next comment catches me by surprise.

"The fact that Betty spoke up and had the silent support of the rest of the WW9 is key. She may be an old spinster, but she is still the matriarch controlling the family's destiny."

"That can't be," I protest. "It's the first time I've ever heard her assert herself at any of the meetings."

Nonplussed, Chet continues, "The fact that she would speak out in a manner that clearly reveals her authority is evidence of how threatened they feel. She's like Don Corleone in *The Godfather*. The less the outside world knows, the better. But believe me, she's a central player in all this."

We finish our drinks and as Chet's about to leave, he asks, "Anything else?"

"No, unless you're interested in a crazy story the fiancé of one of our longtime staffers told me." That stops him in his tracks.

"The fact that you even mention it means I need to be interested." As he sits back down, I relay Albert Consolvas's passionate statement that the current theory that fossil fuels are the root cause of global warming is bogus.

Chet looks pensive. Finally, he says, "I don't believe in coincidences. I'll run a background check on Albert and Shauna."

"We have to assume you're being watched." He hands me a key card to one of the Club rooms. "Your baggage has already been moved. If anyone asks, Crystal will tell them she spent the night with you." Getting up to leave, he remarks. "By the way, your snitch Kevin Riggs calls the same number at least three times a week."

As soon as I hear the number, I know exactly whom he's passing the info to. It's the number of our district office on the West Coast and rings directly to Trent Watersworth.

The bed is great and the pillows are soft, but I can't sleep a wink. The sequence of events over the past few weeks keeps playing in my head like an endless DVD. That and the hole in my heart left by Chloe's betrayal have me tossing all night. If only she were an innocent player in this whole mess.

TWENTY-FIVE

Chet gave me three disposable phones with keyboards so we could talk or text. His instructions were emphatic. "Only contact me on one of these phones and rotate use of them."

On the drive back to DC, I call Emily. Not recognizing the number, she responds with a cautious, "Hello?"

"Emily, it's me, Mark."

With relief in her voice, she says, "Oh Mark, I'm glad you called. I thought of something that might be important."

I assure her that everything is important at this point.

"Uncle Chuck had a cabin up in the Finger Lakes region of New York."

I didn't know that, though I'm unclear why it is important.

With the next words out of her mouth, I'm suddenly focused.

"He sometimes went up there when he was engaged in a deep research project. Three days before his death," at this point, her voice starts to quiver, "he told me he was driving up to the cabin to get something. It seemed odd he would drive twelve hours roundtrip just for that."

I'm already looking for the next exit off the Garden State Parkway. "Emily, stay put. I'll be there in two hours. We're going to take a little ride to the Finger Lakes."

I pick her up in front of her hotel. She throws an overnight bag on the backseat, slides in the front next to me, and we head off. We say little the first hour. Both of us are lost in private thought. As we cross the Tappan Zee Bridge, the gloom seems to lift. "Emily, I hope this is not a waste of time, but your uncle's trip to the cabin has to be important."

I'm not ready to tell her that I hope he's left information critical to unraveling this mystery. "Perhaps there are some papers or notes that will be helpful in understanding what happened."

As we drive and talk, the turmoil within me grows. The pain of Chloe's betrayal stays with me like a throbbing toothache. Still, I hope that somehow she will emerge innocent. At the same time, I realize that here in the car is a woman of special character. She sees life much like her uncle did, though perhaps with a bit less fanfare. Unlike Chloe, Emily is not a chance encounter, nor does she have a hidden agenda. I've known her since she was a teenager. Her grief is my grief. The horror of Chuck's death brought us together, but it's a shared hope that's forging something deeper, at least for me.

It's impossible to detect any interest on her part, other than our mutual desire to clear Chuck's name and get to the bottom of what's beginning to look like a genuine conspiracy. At some level, I hope Emily doesn't have feelings for me as it makes life much simpler.

As we drive through the beautiful, though at this late hour, largely unseen countryside, we review what we know to date. Emily runs through what the private medical examiner told her. He speculated that Chuck had to have been asleep at the time the carbon monoxide was administered.

"But the city's ME ruled it was a drug overdose. How could it have been administered without Chuck knowing?" I argue.

"The private ME theorized someone may have entered the room after he was unconscious but still alive and carefully injected an overdose into a difficult-to-detect place, such as a scalp vein. Even if the county coroner had been alerted to the possibility, it would have been hard to find."

I mull this over but can form no conclusion. In turn, I walk Emily through the sequence of events beginning with Trendle's remarks that cast doubt on his belief in global warming. She knew about my visit with Chuck, but was not aware of the warning he'd given me shortly before his death.

"I'm worried about you, Mark."

I look over and the fear on her face is palpable. Briefly, I consider boasting that there's nothing to worry about. Instead, I opt for honesty.

"Emily, I'm scared to death, too. I no longer believe Edelstein's death was an accident and now with what you've just told me about your uncle's death, we need to be very careful," I say, no longer able to hide my anxiety. "Just a few weeks ago, I was a rising star among the staffers in Congress, chief of staff to its most prominent environmentalist. It's where I'm meant to be: challenged, alive, engaging the powerful movers and shakers. Now I'm constantly looking over my shoulder, paranoid that my e-mails and phone calls are being monitored."

Emily puts her hand on my arm. "What aren't you telling me?"

"There's someone in the office spying on me. I've had a private eye checking him out and it looks like he has been reporting my every movement to our district office manager on the West Coast, someone I've confided in over the years."

Then after a pause, what I had vowed not to discuss comes tumbling out. "On top of all this, someone I care for deeply is likely part of the conspiracy."

Emily, with sincere sympathy, voices the same hope that I'm clinging to: "Perhaps she is unknowingly being manipulated."

"She is working for the WW9 and is, like you, an attorney. Do you really think she's innocent?"

I tell her about the trap I set up through Kevin and how it seemed that Chloe took the bait by offering me tickets to the game a week later.

Emily doesn't respond. But when I look over and see the raised eyebrow and grim expression she is wearing, I have my answer. Chloe's no fool and must be deeply involved.

"I took a look at controversial decisions handed down by the Supreme Court," Emily says, changing the subject. "One in particular jumped out. It resulted in a major jump in the stock price of several domestic producers of oil and one Fortune 100 industrial corporation."

"Was Kensington involved?"

"His was the swing vote."

She goes on to describe a case of eminent domain in which the lower courts rendered a decision and the appellate court confirmed that private landowners did not have to agree to let their property be used for oil and gas transportation pipelines. This resulted in an extended slump in Con-Gen's stock valuation, since a major portion of its business is laying pipeline. By all accounts, it appeared the Supreme Court would uphold that decision in a 5–4 split vote. To the surprise of many, it went the other way, with Kensington, not known as a business-friendly judge, throwing his vote to big business.

That's fine, but how did anyone profit? Seemingly able to read my thoughts, Emily goes on. "An international scandal erupted when it was discovered that a consortium of Nicaraguan banks had bought up large blocks of the depressed stock. When the decision was announced, Con-Gen's stock price doubled within three days and the banks quickly cashed out."

"What happened to the banks?"

Emily went on to explain that Nicaraguan law shields banks from revealing who they purchase stock for. "There were outstanding warrants against the banks, but the Nicaraguan judiciary refused to acknowledge that US courts have any jurisdiction. And the matter was eventually dropped."

As she finishes up, I decide to stop for gas. I have a brief moment of panic when I realize the same car has been behind us for at least an hour, but since it continues on, I push it out of my mind.

We reach Chuck's cabin at 2:30 a.m. It's not a traditional broken-down shanty, but a very modern structure assembled by one of the premier New England builders of log homes. There's little to see in the dark. Emily reaches under the big cowbell hanging next to the door and pulls out a key. As we enter, I'm momentarily stunned. In contrast to the urban blandness of his New York apartment and university office, this could have been the hunting lodge of a wealthy CEO, except for the lack of guns over the mantle.

The room is magnificent. I'm immediately drawn to the floor-to-ceiling granite fireplace at one end of the spacious living area. The hearth is large enough to roast a pig. The furniture is covered in rich leather. Various Native American tapestries hang on the walls. The room extends into a combination kitchen and dining area that could comfortably seat twelve.

Emily sees the look of surprise on my face. "My uncle was very well off and built this place as a combination personal retreat and research center." Noticing my interest in the tapestries, she explains, "He knew the history of the New York Iroquois and other native tribes, and supported local artists from the reservations."

I realize this is a multi-floor structure with a staircase leading to the second floor. Off the main room are a bathroom and an office equipped with the latest PC and web-enabled technology.

"He conducted a lot of research from here and networked with dozens of university contacts around the country and internationally," Emily points out. Piles of papers and folders throughout the office suggest active research was underway.

After scoping out the place, we reach our limit and need a few hours of sleep. Upstairs are a full bath and two guest bedrooms. I flop on the bed in one and Emily takes the other. In spite of the strain and anxiety, I immediately fall into a deep, dreamless sleep.

I awake to the sound of running water. It's 9:27a.m. according to the clock on the table next to the bed. By the time I make my way down the hall toward the bathroom, the water ceases running. The door opens and out walks Emily with glistening wet hair, wrapped only in a towel. At that moment, two voices start shouting in my head. One yells, "Warning, warning, warning! Do not touch! Do not pass go!" and the other whispers, "This is too good to be true." Fortunately, she simply smiles at me and says, "Good morning, sleepyhead," in that goofy way people talk first thing in the morning. She walks past me into her bedroom to dress while I proceed to take a long, cold shower, which manages to chill out some of the wilder fantasies flashing inside my brain. As I walk downstairs, I can smell bacon and eggs already cooking on the stove.

Before I sit down Emily comes close and takes my hand in hers. "Mark you were always my uncle's favorite when you were one of his students. I understand why now."

She draws me closer and kisses me tenderly on the lips. Looking into my eyes, she says, "Back then you were twenty-one and I was fifteen." After a pause, she continues, "In case you hadn't noticed I'm not fifteen anymore."

Nodding my head sheepishly, I reply, "Believe me, I noticed. But—" She puts her finger to my mouth to silence me.

"I know you need to work through your feelings for Chloe. I understand. We were brought together unexpectedly under sad and troubling circumstances. It would be unfair of me to expect anything more at this point. And I would be disappointed in you if you didn't give Chloe a chance to explain."

"Emily, ever since you fell asleep in my arms back at your uncle's apartment, I realized I felt the same way about you. But I was afraid to say anything about it to you at the time."

She laughs. "Good idea. You probably would have scared me off." After a pause she announces: "We better get back to work."

As we sit and eat, we make a game plan for the day. "Chuck's office is where we need to look," I suggest, and Emily agrees. "Somewhere in those piles of paper or on his desktop lies the answer."

She thinks for a minute. "I think I know how to access my uncle's e-mail and computer files. I'll concentrate on that. You handle the paper files." Like all researchers, Chuck was fanatic about intellectual theft, which means Emily had to have access to his password.

We clean up breakfast and make our way to the office. As I begin working my way through the piles on the floor, sofa, and worktable, I can hear Emily at the PC quietly singing, "It's a beautiful day in the neighborhood." I burst out laughing and finish with, "Would you be my, could you be my neighbor."

"Seriously though, Uncle Chuck always told me that if I was to remember any advice it was the theme song from *Mr. Rogers' Neighborhood*. He always said information is power. If you want access, go to *Mr. Rogers' Neighborhood*. I always thought it was just some silly thing he told me as a kid but now I'm not so sure." She fiddles with the keyboard, typing in various passwords, until she suddenly yells, "Whoa I'm in!"

"What was the password?"

"Beautiful Day."

With that, she's up and running. For the next two hours, we work in silence. I create a new but smaller pile of documents that seem relevant. Every so often, I hear the printer come to life as Emily sends another promising e-mail to print.

Suddenly, I stumble upon a research paper that is authored by someone I've met recently. "You've got to see this."

"What is it?"

"Listen, I didn't tell you about this because at the time it seemed to be completely unrelated. But recently, our long-time office manager, Shauna, begged me to meet with her graduate-student fiancé about a theory he had."

"Which was?"

I recount Albert's impassioned plea to reexamine the science of global warming; that it was flawed. "He walked me through the historical evidence and made a convincing argument that much of what we call man-made is nothing more than a phase of the long-term cycle of warming and cooling that the Earth has experienced for thousands of years."

"Could it be related to the doubts Trendle was voicing?"

"I didn't think so at the time but now…" My voice trails off.

Finally, she cannot contain her curiosity any longer. In an exasperated tone, she pleads, "What!"

For an answer, I hold up a folder with the name "Albert Consolvas" printed on the outside and a subheading that reads "Global Warming a Force of Nature, Not of Man." Underneath that, "T. Trendle" was penciled.

Just then, a shot rings out and the glass in the window behind me shatters. I drop to the floor and quickly crawl over to Emily, pulling her down to the floor next to me. "What was that?" she screams.

Barely able to speak, I whisper, "A bullet." As we lay silently, not sure what to do next, we hear a noise in the back of the cabin, followed by footsteps running away.

With that, a strong smell of propane enters the room. Thinking faster than I do, Emily grabs the stack of printouts and points to the pile I created. "Let's get out of here. Grab the folders!"

We crawl out of the office and into the living area. "Whoever it is, they're likely watching the front and back doors," I caution.

"I have an idea." She crawls toward the fireplace with me in pursuit. To the right of the hearth is a four-foot section of hinged paneling I hadn't noticed before. She quickly opens it and we climb into the woodbin on the outside of the cabin, which, fortunately, is empty.

"We should be able to get out this way unseen," she whispers. Carefully raising the lid and checking to see if anyone is around, we climb out and, crouching, run to the tree line about thirty feet away. Just as we pass a tall pine, a tremendous explosion behind us blows us to the ground. Ears ringing, I reach for Emily. She squeezes my hand in return, letting me know she's alive. We're motionless for several minutes until finally we force ourselves to get up. Shaken, with bruises and cuts on the backs of our necks and arms, we turn to see what was once a sturdy log cabin flattened beyond recognition. Stunned, we sit and stare at the ruins for a good ten minutes.

"Let's gather up the papers we took and drive somewhere safe where we can review them," I finally say. As we head toward the car, it's quickly apparent we need a plan B, since all that's left of it is a burning carcass.

"I guess we walk," I say, pointing to a path through the trees.

"It leads down to the lake. Mom and I used it when we vacationed here."

As we walk, our conversation inevitably centers on the fix we're in and what to do next. Feeling around my belt, I realize I still have two cell phones. My own is useless, as it's likely being tracked, but I have one of the untraceable BlackBerrys Chet gave to me. Unfortunately, the other two burned up with the car.

"We have the papers and that's important." Though I wonder, given our predicament, where and how we're going to make use of them. We walk on for a bit until Emily suddenly stops and slowly begins to smile.

"What is it?"

"There is one huge advantage we have here," she says with a twinkle in her eye.

"And what could that possibly be?"

"The enemy, whoever it is, thinks we're dead. We need to take advantage of that without revealing, at least for a while, that we're still very alive."

We make our way down to the water.

There's a bench by the beach. Looking around we can see no one else and hope we're safe.

"I have an idea that will allow us to remain officially dead while investigating the information in your uncle's papers." Using my one remaining cell phone, I call Southers.

"Chet, its Mark Burnham." He starts to reply and I cut him off. "Listen, we are in a bind and need your help." I walk him through the last twenty-four hours, the papers we have, and our newfound status as walking dead.

"I'll call you back in thirty minutes," he says. With that, he hangs up. While waiting for the call back, I provide Emily with a vivid description of the WW9.

She teases me when I mention Liddy's obvious sexual overtures. "Maybe I am too young for you."

I assure her that's not the case.

She's sympathetic to the elderly Rumple Sisters, that is, until I relate Betty's threat. T.C. Clarkson struck her as "a corporate slug," as she put it. Lucas Davidson was no surprise at all.

"Every law firm has a Lucas."

It's when I describe Malcolm that her mood goes dark.

"Mark, he's the dangerous one. Guys as enigmatic and elusive as you describe him are always trouble."

Just then, the phone rings. "Mark, which lake are you on?" Southers asks. It happens to be Hemlock, the westernmost one. How appropriate, I thought.

"Hold a minute." I can hear him talking to someone in the background. Finally, he comes back on the line. "Can you make it to the public boat launch at the north end of the lake?"

I pass Chet's question on to Emily. "No problem. We're ten minutes by foot."

"OK, be there in an hour and wait." With that, Southers hangs up.

TWENTY-SIX

Sure enough, the trail leads into a large parking area that slopes down toward the lake. We stand silently, looking out at the ducks as they lazily paddle along, occasionally plunging their heads into the icy water looking for fish. Dusk is settling around us when I hear the sound of an airplane approaching. A single-engine Cessna with pontoons is making its final approach and lands about a hundred yards offshore. It taxies up to the ramp. As the prop stops spinning, the door opens, and the craziest looking woman I've seen in a long time jumps out. "Howdy, I'm Doris. Chet sent me."

I nod.

Pointing, she says, "And you must be Emily."

Doris looks to be about seventy years old and is wearing a T-shirt that reads "Shit Happens" across her chest. She has on a skirt that could have doubled as a kilt and combat boots with white knee socks. Emily and I just stare.

"Well, what are you waiting for?" she yells. "Chet says you're in big trouble and need to hide in plain sight."

With much trepidation, we board the four-seater and sit in the back. We dump the pile of papers from Chuck's cabin into the small storage area behind the seats. Three times, I try to ask Doris where she's taking us, but the roar of the engine eliminates the possibility of any conversation. With a thumbs-up, she quickly taxies out to deeper water, and a minute later, we're airborne.

Emily and I whisper a few remarks between us, trying to capture the weirdness of all this. We spend the trip alternately looking out the windows trying to figure where we're going and staring at Doris's two, steel-gray pigtails held together by rainbow hair bands and her hoop earrings that are big enough to host an NBA dunk-off.

Two hours later, a body of water that looks to be the Hudson River appears. Doris reduces the power, lowers the flaps, and two minutes later, we're on what indeed is the Hudson, just north of Bear Mountain. Concerned about hitting something in the dark, she taxies cautiously and pulls up next to what looks like a large party boat.

Cutting the engine, she turns and says, "Hey, hot stuff. This is where you and your main squeeze get off."

Main squeeze? I need to ask Chet where he found this character.

Papers in hand, we board the boat and make our way below deck following the sound of a familiar voice.

"Mark, glad to see you made it. I'm guessing this is Emily." Giving her a quick once-over, he says, "Why didn't you tell me she was such a looker?"

Emily blushes. After trying to think of a clever retort, I decide to let it pass.

"Chet, we appreciate your helping us out so quickly. But I got to ask, who is the old lady deep in her second childhood?"

Chet slaps his knee and laughs. "Welcome to my world. Glad you enjoyed meeting Mom." Turns out, Mom's retired Air Force and was one of the first woman instructors to train new recruits on jets during the Korean War.

After relating the events that led up to the cabin being torched, we review what we found.

"As I was going through Chuck's papers I came across this report." I throw the thirty-page study on the table in front of them so they can read the title for themselves, "Climate Change, a Force of Nature Not of Man: Statistically Significant Evidence from the Most Recent 2,000 Years."

Chet looks puzzled. "I'm sure this is a fascinating study in boredom." He's obviously not a numbers guy. "And I can see a connection between it and Trendle's confession of doubt, but why does this rise to the top?"

I relate to him what I shared with Emily back at the cabin. "Chet, it seems unlikely this is just coincidental. Shauna, Trendle's longtime office manager, pleaded with me to meet with Albert. His spirited defense actually began to convince me that there was something to his theory."

I go on to explain as best I can the evidence found in glaciers that forms the basis of the study.

"I agree there must be a connection and we need to find out what it is," he concedes.

We talk for quite a while about the evidence and clues that have come to light over the last few weeks. As we do so, a plan emerges. Emily will pour through the e-mail printouts looking for evidence of where her uncle's research had led him. Chet will research Albert and Shauna's role in all this. And I, with Chet's help, intend to investigate the offices of Becht, Chalmers & Davidson, looking for evidence of the extent of Chloe's, and by extension, the law firm's involvement in what appears to be a campaign to suppress the truth at all cost. We need to maintain the illusion of our demise while introducing fear and doubt in the minds of whoever is behind this, if we have any hope of flushing them out.

Chet has specific reasons for bringing us to this boat. Turns out, it is one of the Circle Line fleet that takes tourists on three-hour cruises around Manhattan. He had helped the owner out of a tight jam and called in a favor. Below deck, off limits to the public, are fully furnished living quarters, including a state-of-the-art computer setup with Internet access via Wi-Fi. Emily will conduct research while circling Manhattan. Once the timing is right, the plan is to have her resurface, call a press conference, and present just enough evidence to cause panic among the conspirators.

Chet gets me a position on the night cleaning crew that services Becht's offices in California.

Chet has a network of people who owe him bigger than the Mafia and, I suspect, personal info in his files that ensures they are eager to return his favors. In preparation for my trip west, Chet hands me back the cash he picked up at the Craps table and a new BlackBerry. I surrender my personal cell phone, credit and ATM cards along with the PIN numbers.

One of his colleagues is leaving on a two-week meandering drive from New York to Vegas with stops at Indian casinos along the way. Chet figures as he makes withdrawals and uses the cell phone, our pursuers will be preoccupied trying to determine if I'm alive or if someone has stolen my cards.

At the most, we have two weeks before the fire investigators determine there were no bodies in the burned-out cabin.

The next morning, Chet comes aboard and hands me a one-way ticket on Greyhound. Seeing the grimace on my face, he says, "Hey, it's either that or a permanent residence six feet under."

"Since you put it that way," I say, grabbing the ticket.

With Emily safely ensconced on the boat, I proceed to the Port Authority bus terminal and catch the early morning bus, hoping to avoid running into anyone looking for me.

Before boarding the bus, I have Greyhound reissue a new ticket that adds a detour through West Virginia. Much to my surprise, I enjoy the extended ride. It gives me much-needed time to think and, more importantly, sleep. After West Virginia, there isn't much to see except mountains, forests, and hundreds of miles of corn, wheat, soybeans, and whatever else America's agribusiness grows.

As I travel west, Emily provides updates from, as she dubs it, the lounge of the Titanic. Turns out Chuck Wilson had been in regular e-mail correspondence with several colleagues. Of particular interest is a professor at Ignatius University in Managua, Nicaragua. This is the second time Nicaragua has surfaced in connection with this mystery. In his e-mails, Chuck asked about the history of several prominent families, including the Prestons. He also asked about any connections to someone named Consolvas.

Chuck's friend, Professor Wan, provided colorful history. The Prestons initially appeared on the scene as partners of Cornelius Vanderbilt and later as competitors, transporting gold-seekers from the Atlantic to Pacific Ocean as they made their way to the gold fields of California and, later, Alaska. The Prestons, it appeared, also engaged in a lucrative side business acquiring (today it would be called stealing) Nicaraguan national treasures, including early Aztec artifacts, Spanish paintings, and statutes estimated to be worth hundreds of millions of dollars.

Emily is still pouring through e-mails, hoping to find something on Consolvas. Chet has little to report other than that he's in the middle of deep background research on Trendle.

The checkered past of the Prestons, while interesting, is a dead end unless they turn up something more recent.

TWENTY-SEVEN

The half-day detour to Birdsboro, West Virginia, is well worth it. Alan Hurdle is five-foot-six, 145 pounds, and bald. He has a lackluster face no one would remember. When he was indicted for securities fraud, the images on TV portrayed a milk-toast accountant dressed in a wrinkled, gray suit, his tie perpetually skewed. He looked honest and humble. He looked like a Boy Scout leader who undoubtedly was browbeaten by his wife. In short, he impressed those he met as completely irrelevant. It was the perfect cover for the foremost purveyor of the largest market-manipulation scheme since Milken's junk bond scam.

I barely knew Alan except for the regular letters he sent to Trendle, and every other congressman, begging them to advocate for his early release from prison. There's no way Trendle or anyone else is going to stick his political neck out for this guy. His scheme didn't just affect the rich; it wiped out the 401K retirement accounts of thousands of everyday people. Thus, he's destined to spend another ten years finishing his sentence. When I contacted the prison to schedule a visit, I made sure my title, chief of staff for Congressman Thomas Trendle, was included, ensuring he'd be eager to meet with me. Hurdle is his own worst enemy in that he loves to brag about how he fooled everyone for so long with his brilliance.

I sign in after enduring a thorough pat-down for weapons and other illegal items. As I enter the visitors room Alan's waiting, as mild-mannered and unassuming as always. He's wearing a grin as wide as the Grand Canyon. Clearly, he believes one of his letters has finally hit its mark. We shake hands and sit facing each other on opposite sides of the table. Since this is a minimum-security prison filled with white-collar wimps, there's no need for the bullet-proof-glass partition. I want to keep his hope alive, and in truth, if the info he shares proves useful I'll try to help him out.

I relay the inference in Edelstein's paper regarding insider trading related to oil, a Dow company, and lithium. "Alan, is Edelstein just blowing smoke or is it possible to conduct a massive manipulation of the stock market related to these items?"

I can see the glee in his eyes as he rubs his little hands together, preparing to lecture a novice on the realities of the financial markets.

"Of course it's possible. More than that, it's routinely done every trading day. The first order of business is to point out that it is not the stock market but manipulation across markets on a global scale."

He proceeds to introduce me to the variety of stock markets in the US and worldwide, as well as commodity markets such as the New York Merc, where oil is traded along with other commodities.

"Manipulation is done across markets routinely, and the bulk of it is legal. The giant candy companies regularly trade in futures to lock in the price of sugar and cocoa. The airlines make big bets on the future price of jet fuel. To a large degree, that is why in any given year, certain airlines remain profitable even when others are declaring bankruptcy. Investors—including the big boys—regularly leverage positions by adding call options to their portfolios and protecting the downside risk with put options. You can even buy annuities that allow you to hitch a portion of the investment returns to market performance using indexed call options."

"So what you're telling me is that manipulating the market is legal," I interrupt.

"Exactly. Every buy or sell decision affects the markets, and when the giant multinational corporations, and mutual and hedge funds buy and sell, inevitably the markets are impacted. Governments do it all the time by raising and lowering prime rates, buying and selling currency, imposing trade tariffs on certain products, and so forth."

He pauses to let it all sink in. It does make sense, and I realize the vast majority of Americans are as oblivious to this as I was.

"OK. I believe what you're saying. The logic is faultless. I guess my real question is: if this is so, why engage in illegal market manipulation?"

"Ah, the answer to that is simple. One engages in illegal transactions to eliminate the inherent uncertainty that comes with betting on the movement of a stock, commodity, index, or market. Downside risk disappears by eliminating uncertainty."

"So how does one effectively eliminate risk?"

"The same way everyone does," he says, grinning. "The way I did, through the use of inside information confined to an illegally formed syndicate." The teacher in him is really kicking in now. "Let's say, for example, your uncle works for New Technologies Inc. and is aware that the company is about to release some revolutionary new software that is sure to crush the competition. Two days before the announcement, he calls you up and suggests you buy 20,000 shares of the corporation's stock. The announcement is made, resulting in a fifteen dollar per share jump in stock price. You sell a day later, pocketing $300,000 profit in less than a week. That's insider trading and that is illegal."

Trying not to look completely stupid, I boast, "I understand that. Members of Congress often have insider knowledge and there are ethics rules forbidding trading in related securities." What I don't say, I can already tell Alan knows: These rules are all too easily circumvented. "A stock is one thing, but how does one manipulate security prices across markets affecting different and seemingly unrelated securities?"

"The means are the same," Hurdle says. "Insider info and an agreement among a select group of investors. In some ways, this kind of activity is harder to track. For example, if Deepwater Oil announces a huge strike in the Gulf of Mexico, this could temporarily drive the price of oil down. The next day, All Air locks in large quantities of jet fuel buying futures. They do this because they know that a month later; Deepwater will announce its disappointment that the hole came up dry. Oil soars and All Air sells all or at least a significant portion of the futures, thus incurring a healthy—though highly illegal—profit. The challenge for those monitoring securities transactions is proving it," he says.

"Alan, believe it or not, I understand everything you're telling me. When you get out of here, you should go on the lecture circuit. The audiences will eat this up." Nothing encourages someone to talk like over-the-top praise. "There's just one thing I still don't get. Your example is a one-time event. How does an illegal syndicate, as you call them, sustain profit over time?"

He smiles. "What's the one piece of advice you hear from every investment advisor?"

After a moment's thought, I say, "Diversify your portfolio."

"The same thing applies here," Hurdle continues. "Many transactions spread across different markets and among syndicate members as well as the front people they employ, reduce the risk of exposure since individual transactions would normally be too small to catch a regulator's attention."

"So where is the exposure risk?"

"Where it always is, greed in the guise of tax evasion. That's what did me in," he says.

At this, I have to risk revealing the depth of my ignorance. "If the transactions are undetectable, how does the government find out?"

"Eventually, the sums of money become so large that it's almost impossible to hide. Bank and brokerage accounts are monitored. You can wire to banks in places like the Grand Caymans, but those transfers are monitored, too. Setting up numerous shell trading accounts offers protection, but in the end, it comes down to one too many."

"One too many what?" I ask.

"One too many times you say, 'One last big win and then I'll retire.'"

Alan provides a lot to think about. Is it possible that Liddy, Malcolm, T.C., the Rumple Sisters, Con-Gen, Senator Plesher, and Trendle are involved in some kind of giant, illegal scheme to screw the American public? It seems inconceivable, and yet the way Alan explained it, I have to consider it.

"Alan, one last question. Are you aware of any significant involvement by the country of Nicaragua?"

Without hesitation, he responds in the affirmative. "Sure, the banks there love to trade securities in markets around the world on behalf of their wealthy foreign clients. They're so secretive that they make the Swiss look like gossips."

I thank him for the information and promise I'll do what I can to shorten his sentence. As I look back, he waves with a pathetic grimace of hope, knowing that there's nothing he can do to assure I'll keep my promise.

TWENTY-EIGHT

Two days later, I arrive on the West Coast and head over to the dingy offices of Chequers Cleaning Service. "Hi, Chet sent me. I'm from—" Before I can get another word out, the foreman hands me a uniform and ID badge identifying me as Carlos Quinso.

"I don't need to know," he says. "Report here at ten tonight. You're on the midnight bathroom shift."

Great, I thought. Cleaning bathrooms is not my idea of a rewarding assignment, and that must have shown on my face.

"You want the job or not?"

I grab the uniform and ID and with a smile, I say, "See you tonight."

Five blocks from Becht's office is a cheap hotel that accepts cash and doesn't bother with IDs. For three nights, I clean bathrooms throughout the law firm offices and quickly discover why I got the assignment. Each partner has his own private bathroom with shower. Rummaging through the medicine cabinets of the mostly male partners speaks volumes about the financial success of Viagra.

On the third night, I'm assigned to the floor where Lucas Davidson has his office. As managing partner, his is larger, with more oak on the walls, plusher leather furniture, and a power bathroom complete with sauna. I'm told to knock before entering, and sure enough, when I rap on his door, a gruff "come back in a half hour" is the reply.

Finding an empty office two doors down and across the hall, I slip in, keep the lights off, and open the door just enough to see if someone enters or leaves Lucas's. Twenty minutes later, curiosity turns to devastation. Out walks Lucas, pulling Chloe after him and into his arms. With a wicked smile, she responds by locking her lips to his. After several minutes of trying to perform mutual tonsillectomies, they finally disengage. I hear Lucas say, "Hey sugar, don't forget the check for a job well done."

As he hands her an envelope, she purrs, "Thanks and not to worry. That boy of Trendle's is, or should I say was, so into me he never suspected a thing."

She suggestively walks into the elevator and as the doors close, she blows him a kiss. I retreat into the office and collapse against the wall, my eyes filling with tears at the extent of Chloe's betrayal and embarrassment at being so gullible. When I hear Lucas leave a few minutes later, hurt turns to anger. I'm determined to take both of them down—and anyone else connected with this mess, including Trendle.

Entering Lucas's office, I move quickly to the desk. Rage threatens to consume me. Struggling to get control, I notice an open folder sitting in the middle of the desk. It contains a two-page report with Chloe's signature at the bottom, summarizing what she learned from me regarding Chuck. I'm tempted to take the report as evidence of her duplicity. However, that would tip our hand too soon. Jotting some notes on a piece of scrap paper, I close the door and quickly leave the office for the hotel. I send a short text message, including the pictures of Chloe and Lucas wrapped in each other's arms that I'd captured on my cell phone, to Chet along with a suggestion. Five minutes later, a three-word reply pops up: "I love it!"

The next day, Emily, Chet, and I engage in a three-way conference call to compare notes and figure out our next steps. I say little about Chloe beyond a bare description of what I'd witnessed. Besides, the pictures I managed to snap through the crack in the door say it all. Thankfully, Chet and Emily are sensitive enough not to inquire further.

While I was cleaning bathrooms, Emily talked with Professor Wan at Ignatius University. His name suggests he's Asian, which he is, but that's misleading. His family emigrated from China to Nicaragua in the 1850s to work the inland steamship routes that connected the Atlantic and Pacific Oceans by way of Nicaragua's lakes and rivers. The professor is a native and patriotic Nicaraguan, who also happens to be the leading authority regarding its history, including its often-tumultuous relationship with the US. He was sorry to hear of Chuck's death and eager to assist his niece. Emily indicated she was closing out her uncle's research on the Preston family. The professor promised to forward whatever he could learn.

Meanwhile, Chet dug up some info regarding Albert and Shauna. As it turns out, Shauna is a stepsister to Trendle's niece, who in turn is cousin to Malcolm Little. The plot's getting thicker at every turn. "We have to proceed very carefully," Chet warns. "With this extended family, especially one willing to kill, they have decades of experience burying the past."

"Chet, did the photos get delivered?" I ask.

He laughs long and hard. "My buddy, another PI, arranged to have a particularly embarrassing shot of Lucas and Chloe sent to Lucas's wife in a plain, brown envelope. We Photoshopped out the background so Lucas can't be sure where the picture was taken. My buddy also managed to get an audio dish focused on the Davidson manor. You would have thought World War III broke out. His wife was screaming and heaving the good china at him. In between crashes, Lucas kept saying, 'Honey, she doesn't mean anything to me,' which, of course, only added fuel to the fire. You can bet Lucas is sleeping in town at the law firm's apartment for the next few weeks."

He adds, "Undoubtedly in the arms of the stunning Chloe."

I wince at that, and Chet quickly realizes his mistake. "Sorry, Mark. I know it still hurts."

He's right. But I definitely need to move on.

As I sit on the edge of the lumpy hotel bed, visions of the Rumple Sisters with AK-47s mowing the three of us down keep popping up. Fortunately, it seems they still believe Emily and I are dead. We have another week, at the most, before that'll change. The challenge is how to emerge alive in a manner that will cause maximum damage to the Preston reputation, without getting us killed. Emily decides to continue surfing the net and talking with Professor Wan in an effort to uncover further information about the family. She lucked out in discovering that the *San Francisco Ledger* is the keeper of dusty back issues of its predecessor, a weekly tabloid known as *The Rush*. Fortunately, thanks to a grant from the Library of Congress, the paper had scanned all back issues, beginning in 1848. It's a historical treasure chest available online.

The Rush was largely a gossip rag sold to gold-seeking transients and local merchants desperate for news of any kind. That's exactly what Emily needs. Sure enough, she quickly finds a letter to the editor dated January 2, 1851, that lambastes Thaddeus Preston, shipping tycoon and corrupter of morals. In the letter, Dr. John Cunningham, rector of St. Paul's Episcopal Church, vilified Preston for promoting his Travelers Clubs in Nicaragua that featured young women of "peculiar distinction and questionable domestic qualities." Undoubtedly, Preston welcomed such notoriety, as it only would have served to increase business at the clubs from eager novices crossing Nicaragua to the Pacific and weary veterans dejectedly returning to the East Coast took advantage of the services offered.

Emily's hot on the trail and eager to continue the research. Over the next several days, she earns the equivalent of a PhD in the history of the gold rush and Nicaragua's involvement. We agree that while she and Chet continue digging, I will engage in some espionage in search of legal documents that lend validity to the research.

That evening, I manage to switch assignments with one of the other janitors in order to get into Lucas's office again. Since several of the offices on that floor are unoccupied, I'm able to skip cleaning those in order to spend more time in Lucas's. By midnight, I'm finished cleaning the other offices and enter his. Going to the desk, I notice the file of Chloe's report is no longer there. As I scan the office, several possibilities come to mind but I quickly discard them. I reason that Lucas would keep the incriminating documents nearby, but would not store them in a regular file to which the secretaries and paralegals have access. Continuing to scan the office, my attention is drawn to the expensive liquor cabinet behind and to the right of his desk. It's a stunning antique framed in mahogany and inlaid with various expensive woods and gold trim. What makes it stand out is that it matches one in the library at Liddy's house. Uncharacteristically, the top's barren. The crystal glasses and decanter one would expect to find are missing. But the cabinet is stocked with imported gin and vodka, single malt scotch, and expensive domestic bourbons.

I pull, push, and twist, trying to find a secret compartment. Finally, running my fingers under the edge of the top, I locate two indentations. I grip the top, press a finger into each indentation, and lift, and the entire top comes off. On the underside is a hollowed-out space containing two legal-size, manila folders. One's labeled Corporate Ownership and the other, Bloodlines.

As I scan the papers in the Ownership file, a chill runs down my spine. This is the mother lode. It shows Con-Gen's ownership intimately bound up with that of its predecessor company, a builder of the railroad across Nicaragua that replaced the intra-country steam line. Controlling ownership is spread among the various Preston family members, with Malcolm Little the biggest holder via nominees; and Trendle, a holder through an illegal offshore trust held by the Royal Bank of Malta.

I'm about to open the other file when I hear the supervisor yell my name. I poke my head out the door as he barks, "Hurry up! We need you to help clean up the mess from the office party on the second floor."

"Be right there," I yell. "Just finishing up."

Grunting he heads back downstairs.

In a moment of decision, I stuff the files down the back of my pants, under my shirt, replace the top of the liquor cabinet, and hurry downstairs. I'm not worried about fingerprints as I, like all the cleaning crew, wear latex gloves. I only hope Lucas doesn't need access to those files until we have a chance to go public.

Thankfully, this shift ends my career as a night janitor. I'm afraid that many more nights of this and I might run into Chloe and Lucas in an even more intimate embrace. I turn in the uniform and ID, and tell the boss that my mother is ill and I have to head east. The supervisor nods. "Tell Chet he owes me one," he calls after me.

Worried, I say, "If anyone asks about me—"

"I know, I know," he interrupts. "I hired you without running a background check because we're short-staffed and when I mailed your last paycheck it was returned because you left a bogus address."

"Thanks."

I walk back to the hotel with the intention of catching a Greyhound back east the next day.

TWENTY-NINE

Our daily conference call results in a change of plans. Emily begins excitedly, "You're not going to believe what the Preston family was into and who their descendants are."

"Any chance they are the WW9, Trendle, and Shauna, among others?"

"How did you know?" she asks suspiciously.

I explain what's in the files I found in Lucas Davidson's office. Walking through each of the documents, Emily and Chet confirm or add to what I relay to them.

"This is serious business. The power and reach of these people touches industry leaders, foreign powers, and government officials, including those on the Supreme Court," Chet notes somberly.

What's remarkable is the extent to which Chuck was able to uncover the information.

"It looks like my uncle's Nicaraguan connections provided much of it," Emily says.

With that, we fall silent, reflecting on the price that was paid to acquire it. Who else would have to die? It's scary to think how close Emily and I are to meeting that fate.

With determination in her voice, Emily focuses us on the essential task. "We must go public with the information in a manner that captures the public's interest and, more importantly, launches a sustainable investigation that is capable of fending off the inevitable congressional pressure to drop it."

She's right. Without a formal investigation, the issue will get the customary two weeks of attention in the press before it quickly moves to the back pages. If that happens, undoubtedly we will disappear as well.

"I know just who to talk to," says Chet. "I'll make a few calls."

In the meantime, based on a handwritten note in the margin of one of the corporate ownership papers, we decide that I will take a quick trip down to Nicaragua. I'd become friends a few years back with Hector Andolpho Rodriguez, Ando for short. We met during one of Trendle's congressional boondoggles exploring opportunities to open up markets in the US for the abundance of lithium carbonate found in the remote northeastern part of Nicaragua. It's easily strip-mined from the vast brine flats found in that region. Lithium is an essential component in the new battery technology needed to support alternative-energy solutions.

Ando and I hit it off right away. We have a lot in common in that we're around the same age and we're both riding the coattails of powerful politicians. Ando serves as principal deputy to the minister of the interior; a powerful position in a country rich in natural resources. We've kept in touch ever since, maintaining a casual correspondence, sharing political gossip, and exchanging holiday greetings.

"Ando, Mark Burnham here." I'm counting on the fact that while Trendle and the WW9 likely caused my "disappearance," the news is unlikely to have reached Nicaragua.

"How's it hanging?" is Ando's jaunty response. He loves to imitate Americans by using slang no longer in vogue in the US. During our congressional visit, as he and I cruised the local restaurants and clubs after a day of tedious negotiations between Trendle and the minister, I finally convinced him that "groovy" is not used by anyone under fifty stateside.

"Just fine," I assure him now. "Any chance you have some free time over the next several days?"

"Sure. I can free up a few hours."

"Great. I'm engaged in some low-level research for the congressman and figured I'd fly down, do the research, and we can catch up over a few beers."

"Sounds good. When are you coming down?"

"I'll be in Managua tomorrow morning. I'm catching the red-eye out of SFO."

His voice is suddenly more subdued. "A last-minute flight to Nicaragua doesn't sound like low-level research."

I choose to say nothing. Finally, Ando breaks the silence. "I'll book a room for you at Las Benz on Avenida Boulevard.

The hotel runs a shuttle from the airport. Call me as soon as you're settled in. I want to know everything."

Fortunately, I have enough cash to book a flight to Managua with a return to JFK. Fearful that our pursuers are checking airport reservations, I find a rundown travel agency in the heart of the Latino district in the south end of San Francisco. The agent looks askance when I request the tickets. But as soon as he sees the cash, whatever doubt he has disappears. By the time these tickets show up on anyone's radar, I'll be long gone from Nicaragua.

Several connecting flights later, I find myself in a two-room suite with a spacious balcony overlooking the marketplace. Clearly, Ando has pulled a few strings. It's 4:40 p.m. local time and a hundred and five degrees in the shade, when a cheerful knock on the door announces his arrival. With a chest-crushing bear hug and booming, "Howdy, cowboy!" we reconnect with the trash-talking sarcasm guys engage in when they first meet.

In truth, our friendship runs deeper. I admire Ando's honesty in a country that can quickly engineer someone's disappearance for embarrassing the powers that be by revealing inconvenient truths. I thank him for the hotel recommendation.

He shrugs. "You obviously have a problem we need to talk about and I know this room is bug-free."

Seeing a tarantula-sized spider on the wall, I know he's referring to the more dangerous, electronic kind. "Government?" I quip with a knowing look.

Looking around as if to reassure himself that no one is listening, he answers, "Worse, the banks." It is well known, though officially denied, that the leading banks control the country.

"Ando, I need your help." With that, I take him through the roller coaster ride I've been on and finish up with a review of the documents I retrieved from Becht's offices.

He stops me at several points in the narration. He's especially interested in the explosion at Chuck Wilson's cabin and asks me to go over the sequence of events several times. "How strong was the smell of propane?"

"My recollection is that it came upon us quickly with an intensity that surprised me. Of course, at the time, we were a bit preoccupied trying to stay alive. Why so interested in this particular detail?"

Ando sighs. "Gas explosions have become something of a trademark with our local hit squads. Several prominent families have lost their summer homes to gas explosions. In one case, the ruling family's ancestral home was leveled and one of their sons killed. He was an outspoken critic of the banks' influence in this country."

"I'm guessing the family suddenly became strong supporters of the banks after that."

"You guessed it." He continues, "The reason I asked about the intensity of the smell is that it is rumored these arson teams pump propane in under high pressure in order to achieve the desired total destruction."

"You're suggesting someone had the cabin staked out in advance?"

Ando nods.

His second area of interest is the family tree. He studies it intently for ten minutes, and then looks up. "I need to get you up to speed on the Preston clan."

I'm not prepared for what he tells me.

"Its common knowledge in Nicaragua that the descendants of old man Preston are heavily involved in our banking and mining industries. Unlike the Vanderbilts, the Prestons chose to go underground and establish deep ties. The more visible members you deal with in the US are related by blood and united by common greed to powerful descendants who remain here."

I'm already reeling, but it turns out he's just getting to the good stuff. "The Prestons and several offshoot branches, Clarkson and Little, directly and through nominees inside and outside the country, built a secret banking syndicate. Because our political system is so fluid, Nicaragua's stability is rooted in the banks."

"But there've been numerous regime changes, ranging from military juntas to Marxist radicals. Why weren't the banks simply taken over?" I ask.

"They figured that out long ago. Much of the banks' assets are outside the country, parked in very stable European and select Asian banks. Even dictators need money. So whenever the banks were threatened by one of our megalomaniac leaders, suddenly and very quietly Holland, Norway, Belgium, Singapore, Australia, the UK, and, yes, the United

States threatened to shut the economy down. Think about it," he went on proudly, "global banking began in 1849 with the Prestons and Vanderbilts right here in Nicaragua."

Trying to digest this new information, I shoot back, "It seems impossible that this has been kept secret for so long, given that it is common knowledge here, as you point out."

Ando chuckles. "The Prestons and their descendants both here and in the US have engaged in an ongoing campaign of disinformation. That and channeling hefty sums of money to whoever is in power at any given time have been their principle and largely successful weapons. The whole enterprise nearly collapsed because of the Sandinista revolution. Officially, Banco Nicaragua was the only bank left while the rest went underground or folded. A great deal of pressure was brought to bear on Daniel Ortega when the foreign banks started pulling their capital and shutting off lines of credit."

"For you law-abiding Americans, the Iran-Contra scandal would have been even more of a problem if it had become known that the Preston family acted as an intermediary between Israel and the US. It was the Prestons who provided the bulk of the money directly to the Contras."

I consider myself an insider, but clearly, I have much to learn when it comes to Central American politics. "Ando, I need to build a credible case against the Prestons if we are to have a real chance of taking them down."

Looking askance, he asks, "What have you been smoking? Haven't you heard what I just told you?"

"I heard. But I need to create a miracle. We need to manufacture a crisis that will mortally wound them and do so in a week." I draw a hand across my throat. "This isn't just politics; it's my life we're talking about."

"Give me twenty-four hours and I'll let you know what might be possible." He pauses, and looking me in the eye, says, "I might be able to arrange things here, but you need to figure out what scandal will be big enough to bring them down while making you look like a hero."

"I'll forgo the hero part so long as we stay alive."

By now, evening has descended and Ando is on his way. Too stressed to eat, I crack open a bottle of tequila, slouch deeply into the overly soft chair, and spend the night sipping and thinking. By dawn, the outline of a plan has taken shape. It needs work and lots of luck to succeed, but nothing else seems even remotely possible.

THIRTY

Managua is two hours behind New York, so by 5:00 a.m., I figure Chet and Emily are up and ready to talk. Fortunately, Chet provided me with a global version of the BlackBerry. I e-mail Emily and Chet an urgent message and tell them to be ready for a call in thirty minutes.

Emily's first words are, "Thank God, you're alive!" That her first concern was for my safety touches me deeply.

"Emily, you knew I was going to Nicaragua."

Southers interrupts. "Mark, it looks like you're being set up. Someone either knows or at least suspects that you weren't killed in the fire."

"Why? What's going on?"

"Earlier today, two men pretending to be New York City cops visited my mother and asked her about her recent flights and any passengers she had on board."

With concern for Emily's safety as well as my own, I ask nervously, "What did she tell them?"

"Don't worry. Mom spotted them for fakes right away. She played dumb and said the only flight she had all week was a lobster run to Maine."

I'm feeling relieved until he continues.

"That's not the worst of it. *The Washington Post* ran a small article about the mysterious disappearance of an unnamed senior House staffer. When pressed, the source would not give up the name, claiming the individual in question had a history of drinking and gambling problems, and that this is not the first time this has happened."

I know immediately what this means. Trendle and the family are setting the stage for me to end up in an alley in Vegas with a knife in my back. I can already see the headlines: "Staffer Burnham Killed by Mob over Gambling Debts"

Thinking quickly, I come to a decision. "It's time to launch our counterattack before I'm converted from an unnamed rumor to a corpse." After briefing them on what Ando is doing, I give them their marching orders. "Emily, you'll surface first thing tomorrow morning. Go directly to your uncle's apartment and contact the *New York Post*. Use the same reporter at the *Post* as before. Tell him that because of what you discovered about your uncle's death, I sweet-talked you into spending the night at a hotel with me."

"What hotel?"

"Whatever you do, don't give them the name of a hotel. You tell him you were so distraught that you let me take you to bed, thinking it would ease the pain." She starts to protest but I cut her off. "Just do exactly as I say. Tell him that once I'd pumped you for the location of your uncle's cabin, I snuck out, leaving you stranded at the hotel. You were so upset that you called your friend and stayed with her a few days. If he asks who she is, just tell him you don't want to get her involved." I advise Emily to show some anger, especially when she gets to the part about me dumping her at the hotel.

Turning my attention to Chet, I tell him, "We need to use the family ties Shauna and her egghead fiancé Albert Consolvas have with the Prestons."

"I'm listening."

"Contact Shauna and tell her I need to meet with Albert on Friday morning. Tell her whatever it takes to get him to the meeting. I'll provide the location later." Shauna in all likelihood is innocent in all of this, but Albert is another matter.

Since he is a Consolvas, and therefore connected by blood to the Prestons, he has a lot to answer for.

I follow up on the lead Chet gave me and call an old friend of his at the Treasury Department. After providing some background about myself, I drop a big hint that the scandal of the century is waiting for a diligent Treasury official to investigate; it's one that will make the Enron scandal look like child's play. Initially, Chet's idea of going to Treasury didn't make a lot of sense. But what had clicked in my mind in the early hours as I lay in bed, straining for a way out, was the one issue that tends to hold the attention of the press and investigators: the American public will not forgive those who illegally siphon tax dollars to support countries hostile to our interests

Albert is a factor because of a small, handwritten line on the corner of the Preston family tree. It said one of the patriarch's granddaughters married a Nicaraguan sugar-cane grower named Consolvas, who it seems, later immigrated to the United States. Mr. Consolvas established what would become the largest sugar cooperative in the US: ICS, short for Intra-Con Sugar. I suggest to the guy at Treasury that Albert is someone worth investigating as a possible criminal link between ICS and Con-Gen. I was going out on a limb with this one, but figured that odds were high that if they probe deeply enough, some connection will emerge.

Albert's passionate and scientifically attractive argument that manmade global warming is largely a myth is the icing on the cake. The analysis is convincing. There have been regular, often century-long, swings in global mean temperatures since Homo sapiens first walked the Earth. While this doesn't necessarily disprove that global warming is man-made, it does undermine Trendle's credibility, especially coming from a family member whom he has mentored over the years.

On the advice of Ando, I spend the rest of the morning at a small library attached to the Loyola Mission House. It was established within a generation of Columbus's last voyage to the New World and houses a wealth of historical documents, deeds, baptismal certificates, marriage licenses, and burial records, along with a collection of books and diaries documenting the Jesuit experience over the last five centuries. I speak with Father Chenko, the elderly resident curator, about research I'm engaged in regarding influential families who played a major role in Nicaragua's history. I mention the Vanderbilts, the Walker revolution, and several other prominent figures before mentioning the Prestons. At the mention of that name, Father Chenko looks up at me and says, "Son, few people outside of Nicaragua know about the Prestons." Lowering his voice, he continues, "You're welcome to look through our records, but be careful; they have long ears." Pressed to explain further, he says no more.

Turning to the task, I realize the impossibility of thumbing through the hundreds of aged books and ledgers that line the floor-to-ceiling mahogany shelves. Smiling, Father Chenko directs me to a room at the far end of the library that houses two rows of computer screens. "We are Jesuits, after all, and have employed the latest optical scanning technology to capture every page of every volume electronically."

He seats me at one of the workstations and provides brief instructions on how to look up information and conduct advanced keyword searches. I then spend the first hour searching for and selecting dozens of documents connected with the Preston name. While they provide historical insight, there's nothing of value to support our investigation. Selecting "advanced search" and using several pull-down tabs to narrow the search, I enter three discrete, key phrases. Thinking through all of the possible connections, I finally settle on the twenty-year period that encompassed the births of the Rumple Sisters.

1-01-1910 to 12-31-1930
Betty Preston
Con-Gen Industries
Intra-Con Sugar

I press "enter" and wait a half a minute before the screen returns the message, "No Match."

Frustrated and about to give up, I try one last revision and change the name to "Elizabeth Preston." Upon pressing "enter," the screen returns a match: Preston Family Trust.

The following ledger entry appears. "1246.98 Preston Family Trust–Executed by Justice Carlos Diego on this day 7-24-1922; trustee Elizabeth Preston."

Subsequent searches yields nothing further. I jot the information on a scrap of paper, thank Father Chenko, and head back toward the hotel.

I stop at a busy café and order a double espresso and a pastry. I lose myself in thought as I eat the snack. With no warning, a smart-looking man in his early thirties, wearing a police uniform sits down across from me. "May I join you?" he asks in clear but heavily accented English.

Perceiving that I have little choice in the matter, I simply nod.

"My name is Captain Enrico of the National Police Force of Nicaragua."

Maintaining a neutral expression, I shake the extended hand and return the pleasantries.

Once he realizes no more information is forthcoming, he asks, "Are you a citizen of Nicaragua?"

At this point, I can continue to remain silent but that would only arouse suspicion. "Captain, as you no doubt suspect, I'm a citizen of the US visiting this great country of yours." With a big smile, I continue, "My name is Mark Burnham. I came down for a few days to conduct some research and meet up with an old friend." Figuring the police have already been watching me, there seems little point in denying I know Ando.

"And who might that friend be?"

"Hector Andolpho Rodriguez. His friends know him as Ando. He and I met a few years back when I was part of a congressional delegation that visited Nicaragua. We quickly developed a friendship and have kept in touch ever since." Again, assuming they've been watching me, I continue, "In fact, he stopped over at my hotel room, had a few beers, and we caught up on what's been going on with our work and families." The captain is caught off guard by the forthright explanation I offer. That and the fact that he's unaccompanied and does not ask to see my passport makes it likely that this is not an "official" visit.

One of the precautions Ando and I discussed was having a story ready should someone ask. I share it before he can ask. "Ando alerted me to a major antique show that is underway this week in Managua. It features Aztec and Mayan artifacts. Studying these cultures has been a hobby of mine."

"So why visit the mission?" he asks suspiciously.

"I was hoping to obtain some background on native artifacts in the earliest Spanish records, but there's little information other than bills of lading."

He sits back in his chair with a thoughtful expression on his face. He rubs a hand on his chin and a broad but eerie smile develops on his face. "My friend, I wouldn't waste your time at the antique show. You will not find anything of interest. In fact," he continues, his eyes boring into mine, "There's a 7:00 a.m. flight leaving tomorrow. I suggest you be on it."

Given Chuck's death and the near encounter Emily and I had, it sounds like good advice. Rising from his chair, he remarks, "Senor Burnham, you seem like an intelligent individual. When you get back to the states, I hope you let Congressman Trendle know how much we admire his work." As I watch him blend into the crowd, the meaning is clear. Trendle knows I've been up to something. He also knows I'm alive and it's time for me to come clean with him.

Walking along the dusty streets back to the hotel, while dodging children looking for handouts from a rich American, I reflect on how much I've learned—and how far over my head I've gotten. I enter my room, pondering my next steps, and I look down. Lying on the floor just inside the door is a sheet of paper. Handwritten on the unsigned note are the words: Little to be learned here. Best if you head home.

The word "Little" is underlined. I know this is from Ando, and the note is both a warning and message telling me where to look next: Malcolm Little.

Before catching a flight to New York the next morning, I fire off a text message to Emily and Chet, indicating we need to meet as soon as I land that afternoon.

The three of us meet in the back of one of those steak-and-ale places found at every major airport to compare notes.

"I was so worried about you, Mark," Emily proclaims as she hugs me a bit tighter and longer than a good friend normally would. As we embrace, Chet catches my eye, confirming that he's aware we have moved beyond good buds.

It's true. Being targeted for death, sharing grief over the loss of Chuck, and pursuing something as sinister as this scandal, has forged a deeper bond than years of casual dating could ever achieve. Gently stepping back from her embrace and assuring both of them I'm fine, I know this is not the time to explore our feelings. There will be time for that, assuming we live long enough to break this story to the public.

"Emily, how did you make out with the *Post?*"

She smiles. "Your friend combines the best of endless curiosity with a healthy dose of sleaze."

"I knew you'd like him. That's why he's so good at unearthing scandals that appeal to the public's desire for drama."

"After fending off questions I didn't want to answer as well as two offers for dinner, I managed to convey the story we agreed to."

"How'd he react?" I am momentarily anxious that he hadn't taken the bait. But Emily quickly put that concern to rest.

"You must have done some big favors for him. He said this had the makings of a good scandal." With a twinkle in her eye, she continues, "I let my anger show as I told him what a bum you were for taking advantage of me."

Doing my best to ignore her warmth as she takes my hand, I say, "Sounds great. Did he promise an article?"

"Should be in Sunday's paper," she says, letting go of my hand.

"What about Shauna?" I say, turning to Chet.

"I connected with her. She was very suspicious at first. I had to relate what you told me about your conversation with Albert before she was willing to believe me. Finally, after much hemming and hawing, she agreed to have Albert meet with me this Friday."

"I need you to get her the location."

"Forget it. She already selected the location, something called the Other Club. She said you would know where it is."

Her choice of venue demonstrates why one should never underestimate Shauna. The Other Club is a nickname certain Hill staffers, twelve of us in all, have given a private dining room at Morton's Steakhouse on Connecticut Avenue, just north of Dupont Circle. We borrowed the name from its more famous namesake founded by Winston Churchill. We meet twice monthly for dinner and drinks and to catch up on the latest gossip circulating through the halls of Congress.

Shauna knows what she's doing. Next door to Morton's is an undistinguished storefront where the Capitol Police maintain a satellite precinct building, offering round-the-clock police presence to protect the many diplomats in the area as they shop and dine. Shauna can take comfort in the fact that with the police so close, Albert will be safe. That and the fact that I'm a friend of the manager of Morton's must have made her certain a stranger would not be waiting.

"Chet, while I'm doing this, I need you to find enough evidence on Malcolm Little to launch an official investigation." I show him the note from Ando. "The connection lies somewhere between Malcolm and Nicaragua." As we get ready to go our separate ways, I lay out the challenge.

"We have until next Wednesday, at the latest, to break a story big enough to expose the Preston secrets, and visible enough to give Emily and me cover."

I turn to Emily. "Emily, when the article hits the press this Sunday, you will be hounded by reporters looking for an interview. Accept only CNN and Fox News and agree to let them film the interview."

Not sure where I'm going with this, she asks, "What should I say when the questioning begins?"

"At first, retell the story you gave to the *Post* reporter. At some point, they will ask if I revealed anything else while we were together." I grip both of her arms, ensuring I have her undivided attention. "You need to call upon all your skills as an actor."

She smiles. "Trust me; we lawyers know how to be good actors when we have to."

Explaining what I want her to reveal, we part, wishing each other luck. We each leave the airport by a different route. Chet catches a flight to the West Coast; Emily, a taxi to her hotel; and I, a different taxi to the Port Authority and another bus ride, this time, thankfully, a much shorter one to DC.

From the Washington bus station on I Street NW and Twelfth Street NW, I catch a cab to Sofitel's five-star hotel on Connecticut and book a room for two nights on the top floor, one that strategically overlooks Connecticut Avenue up to and including the entrance to Morton's. For this, I need a credit card and use the one Chet set up for me.

I spend the next two days watching Morton's and the foot traffic passing by to see if anyone appears to be watching the place on the outside chance someone is monitoring Shauna's conversations. In the meantime, I place a couple of strategic calls to Jack Benfeld at the Justice Department and Drew Nelson at the CIA. I worked with both men's bosses last year, helping prep them for a difficult session testifying before the Energy Committee. They were appreciative of the assist.

I call each of them using the premise that I'd picked up something explosive, but couldn't tell Trendle because he may be compromised. To Jack, I spin a story that Trendle appears to be taking too much money and thus influence from the Prestons, making specific reference to T.C. Clarkson. I figure between the sisters and T.C., someone might overreact and issue a defensive denial. In politics, an unnecessary denial can raise the curiosity of an otherwise uninterested press.

After outlining the suspected Nicaraguan connection, Drew from the CIA is very interested. I specifically mention Malcolm Little's interest in valuable artworks and the suspicion that he's illegally transporting such works to the US. It's generally not known to the public that the Department of Commerce and CIA work extremely closely with the State Department gathering foreign intelligence. It's a shot in the dark, but a plausible one. By linking shipping records to questionable activity, the CIA can invoke provisions of the Patriot Act.

There does not seem to be any suspicious activity at Morton's or at the Capitol Police precinct next door. Friday morning, I awaken at five, shower, shave, and dress in nondescript, casual clothing. As this is the point of greatest danger, I actually mumble something resembling a prayer. Not being particularly religious, it's unclear to me if God is even listening, but what the heck. I throw one into the ether.

The television provides the first evidence that our strategy is working. At 6:58 a.m., a news flash runs across the bottom of the screen during a CNN morning news show announcing breaking news in the death of Professor Charles Wilson. CNN reporter Sharon Claston, outside of Emily's hotel, sets the stage.

"In an exclusive interview, Emily Snow, the niece of the late Columbia University Professor Charles Wilson, told us about newfound evidence that proves he did not commit suicide, but was in fact murdered." She reveals the name of a congressional staffer she is working with, and continues, "We have learned that Mark Burnham from Congressman Trendle's office had been in contact with the professor a week before his death."

Moving from news to speculation, the reporter asks a rhetorical question. "Were the professor and Burnham collaborating on a story? When questioned further, Ms. Snow implies that her uncle had uncovered a conspiracy involving Congressman Trendle, the wealthy and reclusive Preston family, and the government of Nicaragua."

I couldn't help smiling. Emily has played it perfectly. The promise of a prime-time airing of the interview on Wednesday increases the appearance that more is to be revealed. The phones at Trendle's office must be ringing off the hook. By noon, the speaker of the House will undoubtedly summon him to her office for a little chat.

The reporter continues, "When asked about Burnham's role, Ms. Snow shrugged her shoulders and said dismissively, with considerable anger in her voice, that when he got the info out of her regarding her uncle's cabin, he dumped her at a cheap motel. Money appeared to be his chief interest."

To flush out conspirators, this detail was critical to our strategy. If the Prestons, Con-Gen, and the rest of them believe Chuck and I were cooking up a tell-all story, even better. But would it be enough to drive the rats out of their hole?

Emily had done her part. I could only hope Chet was able to leverage his connections on the Los Angeles waterfront. Given that this was the busiest port in the United States, we gambled that it is most likely the place Malcolm Little uses to move legal and—we hope—illegal artifacts and other contraband.

THIRTY-ONE

The time of the meeting was approaching. Two minutes before 10:30, two figures, arms linked, walk furtively through the front door of Morton's. I had asked that Albert come alone, but clearly Shauna would have none of it. Allowing myself fifteen minutes, I exit the back of the hotel and take a circuitous route that brings me to the kitchen entrance of the steakhouse. Todd, the manager and my friend, is waiting.

"Mark, this is damn strange. You care to explain?"

Giving him a you-don't-want-to-know look, I implore, "You're going to have to trust me. Besides, in a few days, if all goes as planned, you along with everyone else will know."

With a look of skepticism, he shrugs his shoulders and leads me to one of the private dining areas. There sits Albert, nervously biting his nails. Shauna stands next to him, radiating an air of suspicion mixed with concern. As I sit down across from them, she's the first to speak. "Mark, I'm so happy to see you. We were all worried that something serious had happened."

"Something has, and I need to make it right." Before she can respond, I continue, "Shauna, I owe you an explanation before I can expect your support."

Glancing around nervously, she replies, "Congressman Trendle is scaring everyone about your mysterious disappearance. He implied you had a gambling problem. But when I asked him yesterday if there was any new information, he dismissed it as a rumor and would say no more."

As she pauses, I take control of the conversation. "I'll tell both of you everything, and when I've finished, you can decide if you want to trust me."

Shauna becomes quiet. She sits next to Albert and holds his hand. He continues to act very nervous and manages to look everywhere but at me. I recount the string of events and what we've discovered. When I mention Kevin Riggs's involvement, Shauna snorts. "I should have known. I haven't trusted that weasel since the day Trendle brought him in."

After I finish speaking, she sits quietly for a moment before asking, "Was the news flash this morning about Emily Snow's interview part of your plan?" I nod in the affirmative. She looks at Albert, still fidgeting in his chair, and then back to me. "Mark, this is serious business and I will do anything I can to help but... but I don't understand what this has to do with Albert."

I look over at Albert. "Do you want to tell her or shall I?"

Looking from Albert to me, she practically yells out in frustration, "What is it?"

Realizing that Albert isn't going say anything, I continue, "Shauna, Albert is heavily involved in all of this, as he is a relative of Congressman Trendle."

With a nervous laugh, she looks over at Albert. "Tell me this isn't true," she pleads."

In a hoarse whisper, he replies, "It's true."

Shauna is stunned and unable to formulate a response. Finally, she asks angrily, "Why didn't you tell me?"

After much squirming and with a puppy-dog expression, he admits. "Trendle is my uncle." A look of shock comes over her face as he continues, "My mother, Angelica, is a cousin to the Preston sisters and married to Jorge Consolvas. Trendle was very fond of my mother, his sister, and after my dad's death, he set up a trust that supported her and funded my education. In fact, it was his enthusiasm for the environment that led me to the field of study I'm now engaged in."

I interrupt at that point. "But your theory punches holes in what your uncle stands for."

"He was very disappointed in me. I've tried to explain that my theory is not all or nothing. The burning of fossil fuel may be a factor; it's just not the principle one or the only one. But he wouldn't listen," he says, shaking his head

With quivering lips and trembling hands, Shauna says softly, "But I thought you loved me."

Taken aback, Albert needs a full minute to understand what she is saying. Jumping out of his chair, he shouts, "No, no, no! Of course I do. Remember I didn't even know you worked for my uncle when we first met?" He says it with more passion than I would have expected from this geek. "Shauna, we are pledged in love to each other. There is nothing that scares me more than losing you."

Clearly relieved, Shauna hugs Albert and begins to cry. Before this lovefest gets out of hand, I call them back to reality. I explain what I need them to do. They both readily agree to help. I decide not to broach the subject of Shauna's family relationship with the Prestons. There is no barrier to their relationship, as the ties were between bloodlines that generations back had gone their separate ways. It was a question of trust between them and they needed to work that out without my interference.

After they leave, I walk through the kitchen and out the back door, retracing my steps back to the hotel. Chet sent a cryptic text message saying everything is in place. I want to reach out for more details, but the three of us had agreed at the airport to keep communications between us to an absolute minimum until we are certain that our counterattack is working.

Monday afternoon, a local news story breaks in LA. Customs agents raided a bonded warehouse leased by US Art Exchange and Nicaragua National Holding Company. Both companies, according to the documents from the law firm, are owned by legal front companies and, at least in the US, illegal nominees controlled by Malcolm Little. The story garnered little national attention, but we knew that would change by Wednesday.

In the meantime, Emily and I need to prepare the trap we intend to spring on the Prestons. It has to be hatched in a manner that does maximum damage and prevents them from coming after us. I decide to switch bus companies and catch one of the discount buses that travel between downtown DC and lower Manhattan. Emily, knowing I'm on the way, finds a quiet place to huddle and work. After a brief hug, we engage in intensive research that rivals anything I did in college.

As it turns out Emily's best friend is the owner of an Internet café and used-book store currently undergoing renovation. It's on Seventh Avenue just south of Fourteenth Street. Her friend is a true iconoclast and loves the idea of her place being used to help bring down the rich and powerful. Working our way through the construction, we go upstairs and set up shop in a corner of the second floor that has a couple of working PCs and a cappuccino machine. Emily's friend, Candy, scrounges up pillows, blankets, futons, food, coffee, and milk. Emily and I organize the files and begin working on scripts to be used when we surface to break the story—hopefully—wide open.

"Emily, you set the stage with Friday's interview. That will ensure that Wednesday's TV spot garners national attention. What we need to do in the meantime is identify and provide hard evidence of Malcolm's duplicity and his connection with the Prestons, the government of Nicaragua, and the deaths of Imlen, Edelstein, and your uncle."

She looks up suddenly and pointedly corrects me. "You mean their murders."

I nod and move on. "Something Ando said offers us an opportunity to invoke the more serious provisions of the

Patriot Act. I hate to risk his safety, but I realize we need his help. We bring Chet in on the conversation via BlackBerry.

"Can you quietly touch base with Ando? We need some information regarding the Nicaraguan arson squads. Specifically, is there any evidence of them handling contracts in the US?" Chet knows exactly where I'm headed with this. Linking them to the Prestons will meet our needs perfectly.

"I've got to work some connections I have within the State Department and FBI, but if there is one, I'll find it," Chet says.

I remind him that we need it by Wednesday. With that, he signs off and we go back to building a case that will stick. I feel badly about tarnishing Trendle's reputation, but it can't be helped. His hands are soiled. The other unknowns are Albert and Shauna. If Albert does as I asked, we have a real chance of taking down this evil empire of dirty tricks and blood money.

My reporter friend, Don, who broke the Plesher/Con-Gen scandal, agrees to vouch for Emily and me with the producers of *Insight into America* a popular cable news show. As a result, we're guaranteed a twenty-minute slot on Wednesday's show. We decide on the New York studio, figuring the odds are better that it's not being watched as closely as the company's Washington newsroom might be.

On Wednesday, we arrive an hour early and spend time with the host of the show, Jim Walker.

"I've got some bad news," he says, looking from me to Emily and back. "You have enemies in high places. I've spent the morning with our legal team defending your story about the Prestons."

My gut is in a knot as he continues, "Apparently their outside counsel from Becht, Chalmers & Davidson contacted our CEO, and presumably the heads of the other major networks, after Emily's story hit the airwaves on Friday. They threatened to sue the network into bankruptcy."

Stunned, I ask, "Does this mean you're dropping our story?"

Jim smiles. "No, it means we go ahead with it. We've been in the news business long enough to smell a good story. If they had nothing to hide, they wouldn't be running scared and issuing threats through their attorney."

"So why legal?" I ask.

"Because we do need to chop out any reference to the rumored arson squads and stick to what you know."

If only Ando had come through.

The show opens with Emily and me alternately reading a three-minute statement that summarizes the sequence of events, with emphasis on Edelstein's mysterious accident and the murder of Professor Wilson. The host of the show walks Emily through the apparent attempt by the city medical examiner to cover up the murder. The explosion at the cabin and our miraculous escape adds considerably to our credibility. Emily says that during her previous interviews with CNN and Fox, she deliberately misled the reporters because she feared for our lives.

"Jim, in fact, Mark and I stayed together and went to my uncle's cabin on Lake Hemlock looking for evidence that he'd found something." With that, she refers to several documents that have already been scanned. A highlighted section appears on viewers' TV screens.

"One final question that I'm sure our audience would like an answer to," Jim says. With the camera focused on me, he asks, "Mark, can you say with any certainty that the Preston family is behind the death of Professor Wilson, the fire at his cabin, or the warning you received in Nicaragua?"

As I'm about to respond, the director begins to wave frantically and draw his hand across his throat. Our surprised host announces, "Folks we are going to a commercial but please stay tuned, as it appears fresh information regarding this story has been handed to us."

With that, the director runs over and hands Jim an Associated Press report that just came across the wire. It announces that Malcolm Little, Betty Preston, and Lydia Van Flugete have just been indicted on two counts of violating the Patriot Act and one count of conspiracy to murder Professor Charles Wilson.

"In my eight years of hosting this show, this has never happened," Jim says excitedly. "When we come back on the air, I'm going to read this to the audience and then lead you through a discussion of the documents you obtained from Lucas's office and the Nicaraguan connection, including the trust document you found."

"But won't this jeopardize the case the government has against them?" I ask worriedly.

Jim assures us that's not a problem. "But," he continues, "the law firm may try to sue you. Are you prepared for that?"

I take Emily's hand in mine and look at her. She nods. Turning to Jim, I say, "We're prepared. What I didn't tell either of you is that my cell phone has excellent video and audio capability and I managed to record everything that went on between Lucas and Chloe as she was leaving."

Jim's concern turns to glee. "Hey, that will make a great follow-up story."

I stop him. "Jim, Chloe hurt me deeply but I'm not ready to embarrass her in public."

He's disappointed but decides to drop it.

I continue, "Her involvement will come out as they make the case against Malcolm Little, especially when they discover that at his behest she went to Nicaragua to arrange the arson hit on the cabin."

That was what Ando found out and passed on to Chet. I show him the message that just came across my BlackBerry, along with the news that a warrant for her arrest has just been issued.

Back on the air, Jim reads the news flash and prompts me to discuss the nocturnal research that led to the discovery of the documents showing the family ties, including the link between Trendle and the various shell companies used to control Malcolm Little's now illegal import/export business. I leave out the part about Con-Gen because that other shoe is about to drop. That is, if Albert has the courage to follow through with his promise to go public.

As it turns out, I need not have worried. Once Shauna sees us on TV and hears all that happened, she practically orders Albert to call a press conference of his own.

"Uh, members of the press," he begins haltingly. "I'm the nephew of Congressman Tom Trendle. More than once he asked me not to publish the studies I've conducted that cast serious doubt that global warming is a direct result of burning fossil fuel." With that, the press goes wild and bombards him with questions. To his credit, Albert does his best to answer in non-geek speak. I chuckle when I see that he has on the same shirt he wore the day I met him.

EPILOGUE

A year has passed and I'm no longer working on the Hill. Congressman Trendle is under investigation. His involvement remains murky but his family ties are so numerous and his ownership stake in Con-Gen is significant enough that his reputation is tarnished beyond repair. He's chosen not to resign, but he has little chance of reelection, since the WW9 is no longer able to support him. Not surprisingly, he's lost all credibility in the global-warming debate.

The Con-Gen connection with Senator Plesher opened a whole second front in the investigation. It turned out the corporation was providing regular payments to EPA and Department of Energy officials to ensure prompt approval for drilling rights to wildcatters and smaller specialty companies mentored by Con-Gen. As oil was found, it needed to be moved to the existing oil pipeline infrastructure. Plesher used her influence along with Con-Gen's money to grease the wheels with Montana officials, who in turn granted construction rights with favorable terms to the company. They generated enormous revenue from these pipeline projects while staying under the radar regarding their ties to carbon polluters.

The GAO added fuel to the fire by releasing Edelstein's paper. As a result, the EPA faces a major shakeup, beginning with dismissal of a number of the mid-level bureaucrats who were involved in the fraud.

Malcolm Little is now in a witness protection program, spilling his guts about all he knows. In return, he gets twenty-five years, rather than life, as an accessory to Chuck Wilson's murder. It turned out the Patriot Act had more relevancy than we thought. The same arsonists who almost killed us at Chuck's cabin were part of a leftwing Nicaraguan terrorist group.

The Rumple Sisters are going to trial for their own part in conspiring to avoid taxes by hiding money with the bankers in Nicaragua, thus violating numerous IRS laws. The tip I provided to my friend at Treasury did the trick. Treasury officials approached the Royal Dutch Bank in the Antilles, which in turn put tremendous pressure on the Nicaraguan banks to leak the agreement between Malcolm Little and the nominees he used to maintain control of vast sums of untaxed money.

Suddenly, Malcolm cooperated and sold out his aunts, providing all the evidence needed to bring them to trial.

The sisters were uncooperative until the US district attorney threatened to deport them to Nicaragua, which was perfectly legal since they maintain dual citizenship. It turned out to be the trial of the century.

The DA accepted my recommendation to have Alan Hurdle review the evidence and testify at the trial. In return, he was granted parole six months later. Alan's now a highly paid consultant advising government and business on security fraud. The public loves him as he waxes eloquent on talk shows, at gold-plated speaking engagements, and in his soon-to-be-released book. The irony of it is that Hurdle also has inspired a new generation of crooks hoping to profit from his experience by launching illegal market-manipulation schemes.

T.C. Clarkson and Con-Gen's board and senior officers are being investigated for numerous infractions, including money laundering, blackmail, and murder.

Malcolm Little's art institute turns out to be a front for illegally moving precious Mayan and Aztec artifacts from Nicaragua to the US. The interesting twist is that within that scheme there was a second, far greater one—apparently unknown to Malcolm—to move cocaine hidden within the artifacts. After Chet Southers tipped off US Customs, they staked out the bonded warehouse and, knowing where to look, quickly tracked the drug ring to Trent Watersworth.

No wonder Trent was always pestering us to get Customs to back off. Trent had secured his position as Trendle's district staff director on the recommendation of Liddy years ago. Trent began his career styling the hair of Liddy's escorts.

Once Liddy discovered that Trent was being tipped by the ladies via services rendered, she threatened to kick his ass out on the street. Trent fell on the sword, swore allegiance to Liddy, and offered to do anything to redeem himself. What came out in the subsequent trial was that she saw an opportunity to develop a reliable supply of cocaine to meet the needs of her escort service's many clients.

By installing Trent in the Congressman Trendle's office, she was able to pull enough strings to piggyback on Malcolm's art-smuggling operation. It was Trent who arranged for Kevin Riggs to spy on me, and he conveniently had Jack, the wallpaper salesman, sit next to me as I flew west for the interrogation by the WW9. Trent is currently in residence at Leavenworth. Liddy was indicted on unrelated charges (technically speaking) of running a high-priced escort service. Ever adaptable, she has managed to avoid jail time by judiciously leaking information that her "ladies" gathered over the years and she kept as insurance.

While I would have preferred that Chloe's involvement remain private, it was not to be. It seemed Chloe was one of Liddy's more sought-after escorts. She had signed on to help finance law school and found out that even after graduation, she couldn't live without the extra income. Once Chloe was linked to the escort service, her involvement with Lucas became known, resulting in his downfall and divorce, and eventually the demise of Becht, Chalmers & Davidson. Because it was well known that Chloe was a friend of Associate Justice Kensington, he was also tainted by the scandal, though not terminally. Whether Chloe and he were more than friends was never revealed, and the protection of a lifetime appointment ultimately saved him.

Sadly, Chloe never recovered from the loss of her license to practice law, the loss of income from the escort service, or from the HIV she acquired from one too many services rendered. She died seven months later as a charity case at San Francisco Regional Medical Center.

The close ties forged between Emily, Southers, Ando, and I became stronger as we endured months of depositions, grand jury testimony, and numerous appearances before congressional committees charged with unraveling the scandal. Chet has become an international celebrity within the ranks of law enforcement. He now commands top dollar for consulting with agencies eager to reengineer their tactics in order to maintain relevancy and funding in this era of unprecedented global financial crime. Because he's a licensed professional, his testimony was part of the prosecution's case at the various trials that ensued. The public enjoyed his unflappable manner and easy drawl as he crushed the defendants with rock-solid testimony. A book he just released, *An Insider's Look,* is destined to propel him into celebrity status worth millions.

Ando, much to my surprise and joy, not only survived the ordeal but also prospered. A number of the Preston clan in Nicaragua were arrested, as it seemed the current government finally saw its chance to crush the hold the family had maintained for almost two centuries on the struggling country. The controlling banks in Europe and their partners in Nicaragua were overjoyed that so much of the Preston wealth was retained by the banks and became part of their cash reserve, thanks to Nicaragua's secret banking laws. It was the bankers who pressured the government to accept the minister of interior's "voluntary" retirement and promote Ando into that role.

Emily resigned from the law firm she was with and formed a nonprofit think tank dedicated to truth in government. Chet Southers, Hector Andolpho Rodriguez, and I serve as the foundation's Board of Advisors.

As for me, it was time to abandon the halls of Congress. I got several offers from both parties to consider a run for open congressional seats, which I graciously declined. Like Chet, I considered authoring a book about the experience, as it would have ensured financial independence for the rest of my life. But there were martyrs in this journey to consider. Connie Imlen, the low-level analyst at TCC Consulting, had died as the result of the paper she authored. A quiet and unassuming bureaucrat-turned-oil-industry-spokesperson was killed because he dared to share the dark secret of the carbon conspiracy. A professor, friend, and mentor was killed to cover up the Prestons' greed. I'll never know how many others were killed, but their sacrifices deserve more than a book.

All that transpired during the past year brought criminals to justice, but did not unravel the full extent of the conspiracy. Several discussions with Chuck's researcher friend, Steven Freeman, convinced me that the Prestons' manipulation and greed is but one element of much bigger, more sinister forces still at work. I'm determined somehow to carry on Teddy's mission, though I'm not prepared to surrender my credentials as a believer in carbon-induced global warming.

Instead, I want to unravel the many factors and power players that are at work as our nation strives to leverage in a meaningful way the foundation built on oil, coal, and natural gas. Like Teddy, I've come to believe in the vision of a bright future based on the ingenuity, creativity, and incredible hope of Americans. Teddy's paper on geothermal energy will be the foundation and launching point in this quest.

While I was pondering my future, Columbia University offered me the chair as Wheldon C. Smith Professor of Political Science. I was flattered and deeply honored. Emily and I talked it over, and she encouraged me to accept the position. "My uncle would want you to fill the position. Wherever he is today, he would be disappointed if you declined."

"And you?" I asked.

"Professor Burnham has a nice ring to it. Don't you think?"

The university was more than happy to put me on an accelerated doctoral track, as the experience of the past year provided enough material to support several theses. One of my first acts upon accepting the position was to collaborate with Albert Consolvas on a paper showing that long-term variations in the global mean temperature was a well-known scientific fact conveniently ignored by those bent on bringing down Big Oil. With me as coauthor, it's assured a wide reading. It was the first paper accepted by and submitted for public consumption through Emily's think tank.

As this unfolded, something else blossomed. Emily and I have fallen deeply in love. It's a love not born of mere attraction—though we are certainly attracted to each other. Rather, the shared sorrow, fear for our lives, and the need to depend on one another forged a bond that runs much deeper. And so it was on a quiet Saturday in May with the sun shining as we cruised around Manhattan on a Circle Line boat, Emily and I were married. We were accompanied by just two witnesses, Chet Southers and his eccentric mother, Doris.

Courtesy of Denise Murphy

28501573R00163

Made in the USA
Lexington, KY
18 December 2013